Spin the Bottle?

'What we're going to have is an authentic, co-educational party," gushed Darlene. "That means boys, music, dancing—the whole works! Not only that, but you can forget boring kid-stuff kind of games like Charades or Pin the Tail on the Donkey. We're going to get the boys to play Spin the Bottle."

"Spin the Bottle? What's that?" I asked.

"A kissing game," giggled Suzy. "Everyone sits in a circle and you spin a bottle in the middle. Whichever boy it points to is the one you kiss!"

"Kiss?" I repeated in horror. "Are you crazy? The boys will never agree to that. Dancing is bad enough, but when it comes to kissing games, the boys will feel just as I do—yuck, yuck, YUCK!"

"Maybe they'll feel that way to start out with. But we'll soon change their thinking." Darlene got this dreamy look in her eyes.

It made me sick. Suddenly I wasn't so sure I wanted anything to do with this party.

Books by Linda Lewis

IS THERE LIFE AFTER BOYS?

WE HATE EVERYTHING BUT BOYS

WE LOVE ONLY OLDER BOYS

2 YOUNG
2 GO
4 BOYS

Available from ARCHWAY Paperbacks

2 YOUNG
2 GO
4 BOYS

Linda Lewis

AN ARCHWAY PAPERBACK
Published by POCKET BOOKS
New York   London   Toronto   Sydney   Tokyo

This book is a work of fiction. Names, characters, places and incidents are either the product of the author's imagination or are used fictitiously. Any resemblance to actual events or locales or persons, living or dead, is entirely coincidental.

AN ARCHWAY PAPERBACK *Original*

An Archway Paperback published by
POCKET BOOKS, a division of Simon & Schuster Inc.
1230 Avenue of the Americas, New York, N.Y. 10020

ISBN: 0-671-66576-6

First Archway Paperback printing August 1988

10 9 8 7 6 5 4 3 2 1

AN ARCHWAY PAPERBACK and colophon are
registered trademarks of Simon & Schuster Inc.

Printed in the U.S.A.

IL 5+

*For Joyce—the most wonderful daughter
anyone could hope for.
And Jeff—her perfect match.*

2 YOUNG
2 GO
4 BOYS

✤ One ✤

It was the first day of fifth grade, and there I was walking to P.S. 373 all by myself. All around me were kids walking to school in groups of two and three. Or, if they were really little, they had their mothers or some other grown-up walking with them.

Everyone had someone. Everyone but me.

I looked straight ahead and walked as quickly as I could. I figured this might make me look as if I had someone important to meet. I didn't want anyone to guess the truth. I, Linda Berman, world's toughest tomboy, felt very uncomfortable walking to school all alone.

Actually, as much as I hated to admit it, I knew the fact that I was a tomboy was part of the problem. Being a tomboy created a lot of problems for me.

I always seemed to get into difficult situations where I had to prove something. I had to prove to the boys that I was as good and strong and tough as they were. I had to prove to the girls that it was better to be a tomboy than a silly, sissy kind of girl.

Sometimes I was so busy proving that I lost sight of what I had started out to prove in the first place. Yes, sometimes life was really difficult.

Take today, for example. There were plenty of girls I could have walked to school with. But they were all the wrong kind of girl. The kind who would rather play with dolls than play ball. The kind who fuss about clothes and love perfume and jewelry. The kind who go all giggly when a boy so much as looks at them. The kind of girl I'd be embarrassed to be seen with anyhow.

Nope, I much preferred to be with boys. Don't get me wrong; I don't mean this in a mushy, lovesick way. I mean the kind of boys a tomboy could have fun with. Boys who would include me in a game of baseball in the park. Boys like Danny or Teddy, who lived on my block and had always walked with me to school in the past.

But this year everything had changed. Danny, who was two years older than I, no longer went to P.S. 373. This year he was starting junior high. And Teddy's parents had

2

pulled a terrible trick. Over the summer they had bought a house and moved out to Long Island.

The only boy on my block who still went to P.S. 373 was Marvin Haven. And he was such a pain he didn't even count. I'd rather walk to school with a girl than with Marvin Haven any day!

Of course I could have gone along with my twin brothers, Ira and Joey, and my mother. But that wouldn't have worked either. Imagine, a fifth-grade tomboy showing up at school with her mother and two little first graders! I would have been absolutely humiliated. No, it was better to be by myself.

So I clutched my brand-new loose-leaf notebook to my chest and continued on toward school. I was too tough to keep feeling sorry for myself for long.

I had covered two of the three blocks between my apartment building and school when I heard someone call my name.

"Linda! Hey, Linda! Wait up!"

Hopefully, I turned around. But my hopes fell when I saw it was only Suzy Kletzel and her little brother, Barry.

Suzy was this round, roly-poly, giggly girl who had been in my class last year. Her brown hair was cut in bangs and reached to her shoulders. Her upturned nose had a sprinkling of freckles. Suzy was smart in school and she was

3

funny. She was even cute in her little butterball sort of way. But Suzy was far from being a tomboy. Not the prime person I wanted to walk to school with at all.

"Where are you going in such a hurry, Linda?" Suzy asked when she caught up to me. She was all out of breath from her efforts. "There's plenty of time to get to school, you know."

"I know," I answered. "I just . . . er, I just want to get there early because I'm anxious to, uh, find out who's going to be in my class!" Boy, was I glad I had come up with that excuse!

Suzy bought it, too. "Yeah, I'm anxious to see who's in my class, too," she giggled. "I'm in five-two, Mrs. Leon's class."

"You are? That's my class, too!" I told her. "Do you know of anyone else who's going to be in it?"

"Uh-huh," Suzy nodded. "Lots of kids from last year. Like Lisa Finklestein and Sue-Ann Fein."

"Oh, them," I said. I was disappointed, because Lisa and Sue-Ann were perfect examples of the kind of girls I don't like. Tall, thin, blond Lisa always wound up as teacher's pet. Her parents showered her with clothes and jewelry and anything else she wanted. She made sure everyone knew it, too. Plump, dark-haired Sue-Ann worshiped Lisa. She tried to

4

dress like her, walk like her, and talk like her. The two of them together were about as disgusting and stuck-up a team as could be!

"What about boys?" I asked hopefully. "Anyone decent?"

"Decent?" Suzy giggled joyfully. "You won't believe our good luck! The two best-looking boys in the school, Harley Silver and Kenton Wolfson are both in our class. Isn't that great?"

"I guess," I answered. Not that I cared how good-looking Harley and Ken were. But they were both good ball players, and that was important. "Who else do you know of?"

"Jeff Davidson. I don't think you know him—he lives in my building. Oh, and Marvin Haven."

"Marvin Haven!" I groaned. "Just my luck to be stuck with him for a year!"

"I don't think Marvin's so bad," said Suzy.

"That's because he doesn't live on *your* block. Marvin's always doing rotten things like letting the air out of my bicycle tires. He's a real wise guy. One of these days I'm going to teach him a lesson!" I pounded my fist into the palm of my hand to show exactly what I meant.

"Wow! Do you really think you could beat up Marvin Haven?" Suzy's brother Barry piped up. "You're just a girl!"

"But not just any girl. I happen to be a

tomboy. And I'm tough." I flexed my arm muscle, which I'm happy to say is quite big for a girl's.

"You sure are." Barry looked impressed.

"Well, maybe we'd better walk along to school with you, then." Suzy gave one of her customary giggles. "We could use some protection!"

I looked at her, ready to get mad at the first sign she was making fun of me. But Suzy's smile was warm and open. She really meant that she wanted to walk to school with me.

Suzy was a girl, but she wasn't so bad. At least she had a sense of humor. And Barry was a boy, even though he was two years younger than I was. It wouldn't be so terrible for me to be seen in their company. It beat showing up alone for the first day of school!

So I shrugged my shoulders as if I were doing them a big favor. "Well, I guess I don't mind offering a little protection."

That's how Suzy and I wound up walking to school together, talking about what the new school year might bring. When we got near the big red-brick building with the tall white columns in front, I felt this clutching sensation in my stomach. All these questions kept running through my mind.

Who were the other kids who were going to be in my class, and was I going to like them?

What was my new teacher going to be like? What would the new school year have in store for me?

As we reached the open doorway to the school, I took a deep breath. Now was the time for me to find out!

❧ Two ❧

Mrs. Leon, our new teacher, smiled warmly as she assigned us to our seats. Her face crinkled into lines that looked as if she laughed a lot. Her brown eyes sparkled, and her short, graying, fluffy hair bounced agreeably. I decided that I liked Mrs. Leon right away, and I wanted to make sure she liked me.

That hasn't always been the case with me and teachers. Even though I do well in school, sometimes my teachers and I don't hit it off. I guess I don't fit into the mold of what they think a model student should be like or something. Anyhow, whenever I get a teacher who doesn't like me, I have nothing but trouble all year.

Last year was one of those years. My grades were fine, but I kept getting into trouble for stuff like talking out of turn or stepping out of line. I got a few N's for "Needs Improvement" in conduct on my report card, which really upset my parents. So I made up my mind to get on Mrs. Leon's good side right away.

The first thing that happened was encouraging to me. The desks in room 507 were arranged in six rows of six each. The two middle rows were pushed right together, forming a sort of double desk. Mrs. Leon assigned me a seat right next to Suzy in one of the double desks.

"This is great," Suzy whispered. "We can help each other with our work and everything."

I looked at Suzy's friendly face and smiled. Since Suzy and I kept being thrown together, I figured I might as well make the best of it. If I had to sit next to a girl, Suzy was as good as any.

Better than Lisa and Sue-Ann, who sat on the other side of Suzy. They practically fainted in their seats when Mrs. Leon placed Harley and Ken right behind them.

Behind me was Jeff Davidson, the boy I didn't know from Suzy's building. At first glance, Jeff seemed okay. He had blue eyes that twinkled with mischief, curly brown hair, and a ready smile. I was about to say something to him when Mrs. Leon stuck someone in the seat next to Jeff and right behind Suzy.

Of all people, it had to be Marvin Haven, that horrible creep from my block!

I forgot about saying anything to Jeff. I just sat in my seat with my hand over my eyes. "Oh, no," I groaned to Suzy. "Just my luck to sit so close to Miserable Marvin!"

Marvin lost no time in starting to annoy me. He poked me in the shoulder with his long, hard finger. It hurt.

"Cut it out!" I whirled around and demanded.

When he saw he had succeeded in bothering me, Marvin grinned his evil grin. "Well, if it isn't Linda Berman," he said nastily. "Too bad I'm not sitting directly behind you, so I could do stuff like pull your hair and get ink on your shirt. But I guess this is close enough to get you whenever I feel the urge!"

That statement was all I needed to feel an urge. An urge to smash him. I know I shouldn't have done it on the first day of school when I was trying to make a good impression on my new teacher, but I couldn't help it. I sprang up out of my seat and put up my fists. "Oh, yeah?" I challenged Marvin. "Well, why don't you try something right now?"

"Children! What's going on here? Are you thinking of fighting? In my room?" Mrs. Leon's voice calmed me down immediately. She was staring at me with this look of shock and dismay.

I dropped my fists. "No, Mrs. Leon," I said sheepishly. I wasn't ready to get into trouble over stupid Marvin.

"Linda and I were just kidding around," Marvin explained. "We're old friends from way back, aren't we, Linda?"

"That's right." I forced myself to smile at Mrs. Leon as I sat back down.

Fortunately, she decided to let the matter drop. She finished assigning seats, then wrote on the board in big letters:

Mrs. Leon   Class 5-2
Composition, two-page minimum
The Best Thing That Happened to Me
This Summer

When everyone realized that what Mrs. Leon had just put on the board was a writing assignment, the sound of groaning filled the room.

Mrs. Leon didn't get angry. She just smiled and held out her hand, palm facing us, as a warning.

"Now, boys and girls, we'll have none of that. I know it's hard to get used to schoolwork again after a whole summer off. I figured a composition about your summer vacation might not be as painful as other things I could have asked you to write, such as a ten-page

11

essay on the story of your life, if you know what I mean."

The whole class laughed. We were relieved to see that Mrs. Leon had a sense of humor. Then we settled down respectfully to listen to what she was saying.

"I don't know if you're aware that class five-two has been chosen as an experimental creative-writing class," she told us. "We'll do all the regular fifth-grade work, but with special emphasis on writing skills. We're going to come up with all sorts of projects to help you learn to organize your thoughts and put them down on paper. But first I want to have some idea of how you write now. That's why I'm giving you this assignment. You'll have half an hour of class time to work on it. If you don't get it finished, you can take it home and do it for homework."

For homework! Homework was something I wanted no part of. I went to work on my composition right away.

So did the rest of the class. The room was silent except for the scratching of pens and a few sighs.

I thought over my summer. I had spent most of it in the city. There wasn't much to write about that. The best part of my summer was the three weeks I went away to sleep-away camp.

I didn't want to write all about camp. That

would take more than half an hour for sure. I thought about the best thing that happened to me at camp. There was one shining moment that stood out from the rest. I started writing about the events that led up to it and how I felt in my moment of glory.

I was so engrossed in my writing that the half-hour was up before I even realized it.

"Okay, boys and girls, put down your pens," announced Mrs. Leon. "All those who finished, pass your papers to the front of the room. The rest of you bring them in, completed, tomorrow."

I was almost at the end of my composition when she said that. I really didn't want to have to work at home. So I kept on writing while the papers were being passed in.

I kept on writing as Mrs. Leon had Marvin and Jeff pass out the new math textbooks to everyone in the room. I would have finished, too, if Marvin hadn't seen what I was doing when he came to my desk.

"Mrs. Leon! I thought we were supposed to finish our compositions at home if we didn't get them done in time. Linda's still writing hers!" he tattled.

Mrs. Leon came right over to my desk. "Why, Linda, I'm disappointed in you for not listening. The first thing I want you to learn this year is to follow directions. When I say

13

something, I want you to do it the way I say it. Is that clear?''

My face was burning with embarrassment. I looked down and traced the wood pattern on my desk with my finger. Somehow Mrs. Leon's quiet way made me feel worse than if she had yelled at me. "Y-yes, Mrs. Leon," I mumbled.

"Good," she said with a smile. "In that case, you'll understand why I have to give you an extra assignment to write for homework. Just a few paragraphs on this topic: 'Why It's Good for Me to Listen to My Teacher and Follow Directions.' ''

"Oh, no! Do I have to?" I groaned.

"I'm afraid so." She nodded. "But you should actually want to. You see it's good for you!" She smiled at me when she said that.

So I had become an example, the first day of the new school year. I could see right then that, despite her nice quiet way, Mrs. Leon was very tough.

I had started out my relationship with her all wrong. I had to do something to get back on her good side. But what?

Then it hit me. I had to do all this writing for homework anyway. Why not take advantage of the opportunity and rewrite my composition? I would make it really great, something special that would stand out as best in the class. That

14

would put me in good standing with Mrs. Leon again.

I made up my mind to get to work on my composition as soon as I got home from school. But that wasn't quite as easy as I thought it would be.

❧ Three ❧

LINDA, IT'S WONDERFUL to see you spending so much time on homework the very first day of school." My mother came into the kitchen and positively beamed at me.

I looked up from the papers I was working on. They were spread out all over the kitchen table. There was one draft after another of the composition that had to be absolutely perfect.

"I want to make a good impression on Mrs. Leon, Ma," I said. I didn't tell her that I needed to undo the bad impression I had already made.

"Wonderful, wonderful. Keep up the good work and you'll have a wonderful school year." My mother put on her apron and started to prepare supper. She took a bunch of carrots from the refrigerator and began scraping and

16

cutting them. My mother is very big on fresh foods. Nothing frozen or canned for her.

"Ma! We're hungry. What's to eat?" Ira and Joey, my little brothers, came bounding into the kitchen.

My brothers didn't look like twins at all. Ira was tall with straight hair and dark brown eyes. Joey was short with curly hair and freckles. Sometimes they were cute and lovable, but sometimes they were total pests.

Like now, when I wanted to concentrate on my composition. "How about staying out of the kitchen so I can get my homework done?" I requested nicely.

Their response was not so nice. "No way. We have just as much right to this kitchen as you do," said Ira.

"And we're hungry, so we're going to stay here as long as we please," Joey added. They did that a lot. One would start a sentence; the other would finish it.

"Now, boys, let Linda do her homework." For a change, my mother stuck up for me. That was because this was schoolwork, and schoolwork always came first to my parents.

Usually my parents took my brothers' side in any argument. The excuse was that I was "older and ought to know better and had to set a good example." Or sometimes it was that my brothers were "younger and didn't understand yet."

Whatever the excuse, it amounted to the same thing. Nine out of ten times my brothers got their way and I didn't get mine.

"Supper will be ready in half an hour," my mother told them.

"But we're hungry now!" Ira insisted.

"We can't wait half an hour; we'll starve!" Joey added.

"Well, if you really can't wait, I'll fix you some carrot sticks." My mother caved right in. She gave my brothers a whole bowl of carrot sticks to snack on.

They made this big production over who got to pick the biggest stick first. They fussed so much I couldn't concentrate on my homework at all.

I tried to control myself. I really did. I mean how long could it take my brothers to pick out some carrot sticks, anyway?

But then, of course, they had to sit at the kitchen table to eat the carrots. My mother didn't allow us to take food all over the house. Since I had no room of my own—I slept on a high riser in the living room because there were only two bedrooms in my apartment—there was no place for me to do my work but the table.

As I was struggling to find the right words to put down on paper, I kept hearing this horrible crunching sound from the carrots. And as I racked my brains to decide whether triumphant was spelled "ant" or "ent," the crunching got louder and louder.

I couldn't take it anymore. "Darn it!" I shouted. "Can't I get my homework done in peace around here?"

"Ooh! Linda said 'darn it,'" my brothers were quick to point out.

"Linda, watch your language," my mother warned. As usual, she stuck up for my brothers. "There's no reason for you to get so upset. They're only eating a few carrots."

Now I was furious. "I'm upset because I get no consideration in this house! I have no privacy. Nowhere to work. No place of my own. I can't even have peace and quiet when I'm doing my homework. It's not fair!"

"Now, Linda, calm down." My mother showed no sympathy at all. "It's almost dinnertime. I'm going to be busy in the kitchen and making noise anyway. Why don't you just put your homework away for now and help me set the table?"

"Set the table? Why can't Ira and Joey—" I began. My mother's warning look kept me from going on. Besides, I knew the answer already. When it came to chores, Ira and Joey were too little to do anything right. I was the oldest and a girl. My mother depended on me.

It wasn't fair, but I didn't waste my energy arguing. With my brothers, there was just one way to win. I would wait until eight o'clock to

19

do my homework. That was their bedtime, and with it came the chief benefit of being the oldest. I got to stay up later than they did. It was the best time of the day.

Despite my difficulties at home, I did manage to finish my composition. I double-checked my spelling and grammar, and I made sure I had written all I wanted to say. Ordinarily, I would have been very proud of myself as I handed it in. Unfortunately, I also had to hand in that extra piece on why I had to listen to my teacher and follow directions. That was embarrassing.

Of course, Marvin Haven couldn't let this go by unnoticed. "Too bad you had to do two compositions," he remarked.

"Too bad I don't knock your head off," I whispered threateningly. Then I turned around quickly, so Mrs. Leon couldn't see I had been talking. The last thing I needed was to get into trouble with her again!

I could hardly wait for the moment Mrs. Leon would return our papers. It seemed to take longer to arrive than it actually did. While we did math problems, Mrs. Leon corrected the few compositions which, like mine, had been done for homework. By the time we were finished, so was she.

"Well, boys and girls," Mrs. Leon announced. "I'm going to hand back your papers right away. I marked them not only for spelling and grammar, but for the way you organized your ideas, told a story, and made your point. I want you to learn to introduce your main idea in the very first paragraph. Then I want you to build on and explain your idea in additional paragraphs and come to a good conclusion at the end. I want you to be very clear about what you are saying. When I read your writing, I want to be convinced of your ideas, even if I don't agree with them.''

Mrs. Leon gazed around the room to make sure she had our attention. She did. There was something about her gentle manner that was very powerful. You actually *wanted* to hear what she had to say. Besides, our class had a lot of good students in it. We realized that it really was important to learn how to write a good composition.

''Now, I'm sorry to say that some of you don't have the slightest idea how to write,'' Mrs. Leon continued. ''At this point, I'm not upset about that. However, I expect you to work on your skills so that you'll soon be writing as well as any fifth grader. Most of you are somewhere in the middle. You have an idea of how to write, but you're not quite there yet. And then there are a few of you who are already writing excellent, well-organized compositions. I expect you to keep up the good work and show improvement this year as well.''

Mrs. Leon picked up the stack of papers from her desk. "Before I give back your papers, I want you to listen to some excellent compositions from your classmates. Pay careful attention to what makes these compositions so good. Let's see now . . ."

The whole class waited for her to call out the name of the person who wrote the best composition. "Here's the one—Steven Warshinsky. Will you please come up and read everyone your wonderful composition?"

"Steven Warshinsky! I should have known," I groaned to Suzy.

"Yeah. No one else has a chance when Steven's around." She shook her head disgustedly.

Steven practically bounced out of his seat. Mrs. Leon had put him in the first row because he was the shortest kid in the class. He had a square head that looked as if it had been sat on and flattened. But obviously his brains hadn't been affected at all. Steven was always the smartest kid in the class.

Everyone had to suffer through listening to Steven's composition. And I do mean suffer. I don't care how well structured his writing was—it was boring! Who cared if the best thing that happened to him this summer was learning to program his new computer, anyway? I practically fell asleep listening to him.

I was jolted awake by hearing my own name called. "Linda. Linda Berman. Will you come up here and read your composition to the class?''

"Me?" I sprang out of my seat, trying to look as if I had been wide awake and paying attention. I fooled no one. The whole class was laughing as I stumbled up to the front of the room. I didn't care. I was on my way to getting on Mrs. Leon's good side!

"Nice work, Linda." Mrs. Leon smiled as she handed me my paper. "Read it so everyone can hear you."

"Sure, Mrs. Leon." I took my paper and began to read. " 'The best thing that happened to me this summer was winning the tree-climbing contest in camp.' "

I told all about how Camp Winnepeg had the best trees for climbing in the world. About how I loved to climb trees, see the sun shining through the highest leaves, get a fantastic view of the whole camp. About how tree climbing was against camp rules so I had to do it on the sneak. About how there was this boy in camp who couldn't stand girls doing better than him in anything. About how he challenged me to a tree-climbing contest one night when the moon was full and the counselors were asleep. About how I beat him easily, and we got caught and in trouble, but what mattered was that everyone knew that I, Linda Berman, was the best tree climber in camp!

When I finished reading I was glad to see

that everyone was listening intently, not bored to death, as they had been while listening to Steven. It had been worth all the time and effort I had put into my composition.

"Good reading," commented Mrs. Leon. "And now, boys and girls, I'll pass out your papers so you can look over my corrections."

"Great story, Linda," Suzy whispered as I returned to my seat.

"That's a made-up story if I ever heard one," Marvin commented.

That was too much for me to bear. "What do you mean, made-up story?" I demanded.

"I mean there's no way a girl like you could beat a boy in a tree-climbing contest, and I know it. I myself could beat you any day."

"That's what you think, Marvin! I won that contest and everyone in camp knew it. Any time you want to challenge me to a contest, I'll prove it to you, too!"

"How about Saturday afternoon, in the back of the park?" Jeff Davidson piped up.

I glared at him. Who was he to butt in to my affairs? I didn't really want to have a contest with Marvin. Whenever I had anything to do with him, it meant nothing but trouble.

But I couldn't say no. While Mrs. Leon was busy giving out papers in the back of the room, big-mouth Jeff was already whispering to Harley about the big event. Then Suzy told Lisa, who told Sue-Ann.

Before I realized what was happening, it was all arranged. Saturday at 1:00 P.M. in the back of the park. To be witnessed by a bunch of the boys and a bunch of the girls. The contest to prove who was the best tree climber in the neighborhood. Marvelous Marvin Haven, the boy who had to be the world's biggest pest, versus Linda Berman, the world's greatest tomboy.

⋘ Four ⋙

IF I HAD had a picnic or something I really wanted to do on Saturday, it would have rained for sure. But now that I needed some rain to get me out of this contest with Marvin, the day dawned sunny and perfectly clear.

I stayed in bed a long time, trying to will myself some sort of illness. Nothing big, of course. Just a small stomachache or even a sore throat. Just enough for my mother to say I had to stay in bed to recuperate.

Nothing. About the only pains I could muster were my brothers. They kept yelling at me to get out of bed so they could come into the living room to watch their dumb cartoons on TV.

So, at 12:45, when Suzy called for me, I hadn't come up with an excuse to get out of this contest. It looked as if I was going to have to go to the park and meet Marvin's challenge. Not that I didn't think I could beat him easily. But Marvin was such a sneak, you could never tell what tricks he would try in order to win. And what if something went wrong and I lost the contest? I would never live it down.

"All ready, Linda?" Suzy asked cheerfully.

"I guess," I said glumly. "See you later, Ma. Suzy and I are going to the park," I called to my mother. Quickly, I started out the door.

I wasn't quick enough. As soon as my mother heard I was going to the park, she insisted I take Ira and Joey with me.

My brothers were the last people I wanted to know about the tree-climbing contest. I deposited them in the front of the park where there was a playground with swings and all that stuff. I told them that if they dared to come looking for me, I would take them back home immediately. Then Suzy and I left for the back of the park where there was a hill, a field, and a clump of trees.

Washington Heights, the part of New York City where we lived, was a neighborhood of big apartment buildings five and six stories high. The park was about the only place you could find grass and some decent trees.

It was under the trees that we found them. They were standing in two separate groups. The girls. The boys. And they were all waiting for me.

27

The girls were Lisa and Sue-Ann. With them was their friend, Rena Widmark, who was even more of a pain than they were. Rena had this fat pair of legs she thought were just gorgeous. She would run her hands up and down her legs and say dumb things like, "Look at my shapely legs!" It was disgusting. And to think these were the girls I was here to represent!

The boys, except for Marvin, were all okay. Harley and Ken were good ball players. Jeff was, too, and he had a good sense of humor as well. I liked the boys. I wanted to be friends with them. So how did I wind up going against them in this contest in order to prove something for these girls?

"Here she is! See? We knew she would show up. She'll prove girls are best!" Sue-Ann, Lisa, and Rena squealed when they saw me.

"Well, Marvin, it looks like she didn't chicken out after all," Jeff said.

Marvin shrugged. "I didn't think she would. Linda's always got to prove something."

"And you don't, Miserable Marvin?" I said angrily. "You're the one who challenged me in the first place."

"I had to. After you wrote that lying, bragging composition!"

"It was not lying and bragging! It was true—every word of it!"

"Well, that's what we're here to find out,"

said Harley. "We were just discussing rules when you got here."

"Rules? What rules?"

"Well, as you see, there's only one tree here that's good for climbing," Ken pointed out.

I looked and saw he was right. The boys were under the only decent tree. The others were either too small or had branches that started too high to reach.

"So the question is whether you should climb it together or one at a time," said Jeff.

"We can't climb together. We'd get in each other's way," I insisted. "We've got to go up one at a time."

"Then how will you know who's the winner?" shapely-legs Rena asked.

"I've got a stopwatch." Jeff pointed to his wrist. "I'll time each of you. The one who makes it highest, the fastest, is the winner."

"I'll watch Jeff watch his watch," Sue-Ann volunteered. She gazed adoringly at Jeff. Everyone could see she liked him, but that didn't seem to bother Sue-Ann.

Marvin and I tossed a coin to see who would go first. I won. I had my choice. What was I going to do?

If I went last, I could learn from watching Marvin climb. I would know just how to pace myself. But the chances were greater my brothers would get tired of the playground by then and come back to find me climbing the tree. I didn't want that to happen.

"I'll go first," I decided.

"Yay! Girls are always first!" the girls cheered.

"Boo," said the boys.

I frowned. I wasn't happy with this situation at all. If I won, the boys would be mad at me. If I lost, I would look like a fool.

But I had no choice but to go ahead. I stepped back and looked over the tree with care. I mentally took note of all the branches and planned out just how to make my climb.

"I'm ready," I announced finally.

The whole crowd gathered around the tree. Every eye was focused on me as I grabbed on to the lowest branch.

Jeff checked his stopwatch. "Ready . . . on your mark . . . get set . . . go!" he shouted.

I was off. Taking a huge swing for momentum, I managed to hoist myself up to the first branch. I reached up to the one above it and pulled myself to my feet. From there I scrambled up to the place where the tree forked.

I tackled the sturdier section of the tree next. It wasn't quite as tall as the other section, but the thickness of the branches made me feel I could get up higher. Then, as I attempted to get to the next level, a branch broke and my foot slipped. I tipped forward and saw the ground looming toward me! Quickly, I grabbed another branch with both hands. I was safe!

My heart was pounding, but after that it was all easy. I made it up as high as I dared without further problems.

"I'm up! Stop the clock!" I yelled.

Now my heart was beating joyfully. I had made good time—I knew I had. And there was nothing better than being up here at the top of the tree. Me, the birds, the squirrels, and the great blue sky that stretched out to touch the buildings surrounding the park. It was a wonderful moment of triumph.

It lasted until I looked down. For there on the ground was not the wildly cheering group of kids I expected to see, but a very subdued crew. In their midst I could see the green uniform and shining bald head of Mr. Mancuso, the park attendant.

No wonder everyone was so quiet. Even from way up in the tree I could tell he was angry. His face grew red as he shouted up at me. "Hey, kid! What do you think you're doing up there? Get down from that tree this instant!"

From the looks of things I was in big trouble. Slowly, I began my descent from the tree.

It wasn't until I had both feet on the ground that I dared look at anybody. The girls looked frightened. The boys were trying to look tough. Marvin was grinning this dumb, sheepish grin.

I could tell that Mr. Mancuso had just given it to all of them.

But he saved the worst of it for me. I got this whole angry lecture about how the trees in the park were not for climbing, but for the enjoyment of the public. Didn't I have respect for public property? Not only that but I could have been severely injured or even killed, climbing trees that way.

By this time, a crowd of onlookers was gathering around us. It was so embarrassing to have everyone watch me being bawled out like that. And to think that Marvin, who had started this whole mess, was getting away scot-free! Now he'd never have to climb the tree at all. I had to go through all this without even having the chance to prove I was best!

The worst of it was that my brothers, attracted by the crowd, ignored my threats and showed up. They arrived just in time to hear Mr. Mancuso say that he ought to call my parents right now.

Fortunately, he didn't. He seemed to get enough satisfaction out of making a scene and blowing off steam. After making me promise never to climb a tree in his park again, he let me go home.

"If I ever catch you doing something like this again, you'll be banned from this park forever," he called after me as I grabbed my brothers, one by each hand, and headed out of the park as fast as I could.

"If you say a word about this to Ma, I'll never take you anywhere ever again," I warned them.

"Okay, okay," they promised.

"Hey, Linda! Wait up a minute!" Suzy called.

I turned and waited for her to catch up to me, even though I was afraid of what she might say about my blowing the contest.

But Suzy didn't think I had blown anything. "Gee, Linda, you were great!" she gushed. "I couldn't believe how quickly you made it up that tree!"

Then Lisa, Sue-Ann, and Rena came after us. "You really showed those boys a thing or two, Linda!" Lisa said.

"That Marvin was so frightened when he saw you get up there so fast he was shivering in his shoes!" noted Sue-Ann.

"You never saw anyone as relieved to see Mr. Mancuso show up as Marvin was," added Rena. "Mr. Mancuso saved him from looking like an absolute fool, and everyone knows it!"

"Even the boys?" I asked, astonished.

"Especially the boys," giggled Suzy. "Although they'll never admit it, of course."

I could have hugged Suzy. And even Lisa, Sue-Ann, and Rena looked good to me right then. That's when I decided that maybe it wasn't so terrible to be the champion of the girls after all.

Now I was actually looking forward to seeing Marvin on Monday morning. I couldn't wait to let him know that I knew that everyone else knew he could never have climbed that tree as fast as I did.

⊰ Five ⊱

THE FIRST THING I did when I saw Marvin in school on Monday was to rub it in how I had conclusively demonstrated that a girl could climb a tree as well as a boy could any day. Unfortunately, Mrs. Leon cut my moment of triumph short. She quieted us down and began describing what was to be our biggest project of the school year—the creation of a story hour for the younger grades.

Mrs. Leon explained that this meant we would write and illustrate stories of our own. Eventually, we would go into the first- and second-grade classrooms and read our stories to the children. As she finished saying this, the door to our room opened unexpectedly.

There stood Mr. Wohl, the bald, bristly, and much-feared principal of P.S. 373. With him was a tall girl with long reddish hair. The whole

35

class eyed her suspiciously as she followed Mr. Wohl into our room.

"Boys and girls," his deep voice boomed, "this is your new classmate, Darlene Mason. Darlene has just moved into the neighborhood and couldn't register until today. Darlene wants to be a journalist, and since this is the creative-writing class, we've placed her here. Now, I expect you all to make her feel welcome."

Mr. Wohl went over to talk to Mrs. Leon and give her some paperwork. Darlene was left standing on display in front of the room.

And what a display she made, too! Darlene might have been a fifth grader like the rest of us, but she had a real figure. I mean a woman's figure—hips, waist, fully developed breasts. The whole works!

Even with Mr. Wohl around, you could see that Darlene had created quite a stir just by standing there. The boys were all whispering among themselves, and the girls were giggling to one another. Darlene blushed beet-red. She knew she was the subject of everyone's conversation.

I felt sorry for her. Not that Darlene was the type of girl I'd expect to be friends with or anything. But I could imagine how tough it must be to be the new girl in school under any circumstances. And to be built like Darlene on top of everything else—now, that was really tough!

Mrs. Leon spotted Darlene's discomfort right away. She kept trying to break away from Mr. Wohl. He kept right on talking. Finally, he took the hint and left the room. Mrs. Leon gave a sigh of relief and walked over to where Darlene was standing unhappily.

"Well, Darlene," she said with a comforting smile. "We want to welcome you to class five-two. We hope you'll be happy here with us. I'm going to seat you next to someone who can help you get adjusted. Let's see . . . I know, Suzy!"

Mrs. Leon positively beamed as she made the decision that Suzy was the perfect one to make Darlene feel at home. She was probably right, too, because Suzy was warm and friendly to everyone. But I didn't like what came next.

"Suzy, I know you're just the one to help Darlene. But you really should sit together. Let's see . . . Linda, would you mind changing your seat?"

Mind? Of course I would mind. Suzy was the only girl I liked in the whole class. Not being able to sit next to her would make school unbearable for me. "Well, uh, I—uh, you see—" I fumbled, trying to come up with some excuse that would keep Mrs. Leon from separating us.

"Linda's trying to say the two of us work well together," Suzy came to my assistance.

"We do, and it just wouldn't be right to separate us." I looked pleadingly at Mrs. Leon, praying she would understand and change her mind.

One thing about Mrs. Leon, she has a heart. Any other teacher would have separated us without caring at all how we felt. But not Mrs. Leon.

"Well, if that's the case, I'll seat Darlene on the other side of Suzy. You won't mind moving behind Harley, will you, Lisa?" she asked sweetly.

"Why, not at all, Mrs. Leon." Of course, Lisa took full advantage of this chance to score points with Mrs. Leon. She gave a big smile of cooperation as she gathered her belongings from her desk. In the short time since school had started, Lovely Lisa had already become one of Mrs. Leon's favorites.

And I knew Lisa was just thrilled to sit behind Handsome Harley. This way she could spend all day staring at the back of his head!

I allowed none of this to bother me. I was too grateful to keep my seat next to Suzy.

What did bother me was the fact that Darlene took up so much of Suzy's attention, asking questions about this and that. Also, Darlene made me feel uncomfortable. It was hard enough for me to deal with the ordinary girls in our class. I had no idea what to say to a girl not yet eleven who looked at least fourteen!

If I didn't know how to act around Darlene, no one else did either. Aside from Suzy, Darlene spoke to no one in our class unless she had to. She went about her business looking straight ahead so she wouldn't have to meet anyone's eye. When school was over, she was the first to leave the room so she wouldn't have to walk home with anyone. She was a real loner.

One morning, while Suzy and I were walking to school together, we spotted Darlene walking by herself. She had just turned the corner onto Fort Washington Avenue, the street that led to our school.

"Looks like Darlene must live on One hundred seventy-fifth Street," I said to Suzy. "Only a block away from me."

"Looks that way," agreed Suzy. "Which means she could walk part way to school with us if she wanted to."

"If she wanted to? Well, what about us? Do we want to walk to school with her?"

"Why not?" Suzy shrugged. "I don't think Darlene is so bad. She's just shy about being new in school."

"I don't think she's shy. I think she's stuck-up. Darlene thinks she's better than us because she looks older.''

"Aw, come on, Linda. Let's give her a chance. I'm going to call to her to wait up for us so we can walk with her, okay?"

"Okay," I sighed. "Although it's against my better judgment."

Suzy was already calling out to Darlene. Darlene turned around. When she saw us, she looked both surprised and frightened. But she waited for us to catch up to her.

"Hi, Darlene!" Suzy bubbled. "Do you live on this street?"

"Uh-huh. In that building in the middle of the block." She pointed out an apartment house on 175th Street.

"Then you're really close to us," Suzy said with a big smile. "Linda lives on One hundred seventy-sixth Street, and I live just one block farther uptown. We could walk together to school all the time!"

I could have kicked Suzy! Agreeing to have Darlene walk with us this morning was one thing. Making a commitment for "all the time" was something else! I flashed Suzy my dirtiest look. She was so busy babbling to Darlene that she didn't even notice.

"Linda and I meet at eight-twenty every morning. If you're on your corner at eight twenty-three, we could pick you up on the way. It should work out perfectly!"

Perfectly? Says who? I wanted to ask. But I held it in. Darlene looked too grateful and Suzy too happy for me to say anything to ruin it right now. I'd have to think of something to get us out of this commitment in the future. Maybe talk to Suzy later, when Darlene wasn't around.

For now I just looked straight ahead and glumly listened to Suzy and Darlene chatter away as we walked to school. I had never heard Darlene say so much before. She was talking about how hard it had been for her to pack up and leave her friends in the old neighborhood. Her parents had moved to Washington Heights because the commute to the city was easier for her father. But she had been very lonely since the move. She didn't even have brothers or sisters to talk to. Her mother worked, too, so most of the time she was all alone.

As I listened, my angry feelings left me. It sounded as if Suzy had been right. Darlene wasn't stuck-up; she was just shy and lonely. Look how she opened up just because Suzy was nice to her. I began to feel ashamed of myself for not being nicer, too.

"What do you think of Mrs. Leon, Darlene?" I asked.

"Mrs. Leon? I think she's fantastic!" Darlene smiled now, and for the first time I noticed how pretty she was. She had long-lashed eyes that were flecked with green. And she had this cute little upturned nose.

I had always admired little noses, because mine was one size too big for my face. Fortunately, I had big blue eyes to help make up for that. And I had a normal sized and shaped body. Not like Darlene's, with all those awful bulges and curves.

"I don't think I ever had a teacher so nice," Darlene said. "She really endeavored to ease my adjustment."

Endeavored? Ease her adjustment? Why was Darlene sticking all these big words into her sentences? I looked at her suspiciously, but Darlene didn't seem to notice what she was doing. I decided she wasn't trying to show off or anything. It was just Darlene's way of talking.

"Mrs. Leon makes you like her so much you actually want to do her assignments to please her," Darlene pointed out.

"You know, that's exactly how I feel," I agreed. "Too bad more teachers don't take her approach. School would be a lot more pleasant for all of us kids."

"Maybe we should make her principal," suggested Suzy. "Instead of that yucky Mr. Wohl."

"Yuck! That wouldn't work," I pointed out. "Because then we wouldn't have her in our classroom. We'd have Mr. Wohl."

"Mr. Wohl?" Darlene screwed up her face. "That would be positively abominable!"

"Abominable?" I questioned.

"Yeah, abominable. You know—yucky!" Darlene laughed when she said this, and I couldn't help laughing, too. Suzy joined in, and that's when I realized that maybe having three of us to walk to school together wasn't so bad after all.

~§ Six §~

I<small>T BECAME A</small> ritual—Suzy, Darlene, and I meeting every morning, at lunchtime, then again when school let out. Sometimes Sue-Ann and Rena, who lived in our direction, walked with us. Lisa, who lived on the opposite side of the school, would join us on days she went home with Sue-Ann, her best friend.

I still wasn't overly fond of their company, but I put up with it. Sometimes I even had to admit that it was fun to be with a whole crowd of girls.

The most fun was usually when the boys joined us. Harley and Ken both lived in our direction. So did Jeff and, of course, Miserable Marvin.

Most of the time the boys would start out in a group by themselves. Then one of them would say something fresh to one of us or "accidentally" bump into us. Pretty soon everyone would be getting into it. We'd be tripping one another, throwing books on the ground, whacking one another in the behind, chasing one another up the street.

I'm not sure this was a tomboy way to act around boys. It certainly wasn't the way I used to deal with them before. But I have to admit that most of the time, fooling around with the boys was really a lot of fun.

Except for the day of the Halloween party, an event we all had been looking forward to. The way it turned out wasn't fun at all.

The day started out just fine. It was warm for the end of October. This meant that we could wear our costumes without having to put jackets over them. Mrs. Leon promised that if we got our work done in the morning, we could have the entire afternoon for a Halloween party. She was going to let us wear our costumes to school and everything.

I don't think anyone could have worked harder than our class did that morning. But the payoff was worth it. How often did we get an opportunity to party all afternoon?

My costume was something I had been working on a long time. It was a dragon, made out of paper. I had cut up this paper bag for the head and painted a horrible dragon face in greens, oranges, reds, and yellows. Then I used a large sheet of wrapping paper for the body and painted it to match.

I tried it on for my brothers before I left, to see the effect it would have on them. I should have known better.

"Yuck! What kind of a costume is that?" said Ira.

"Everyone's going to know you made it yourself," said Joey. "Who wants a home-made costume?"

"I do," I said proudly. "Half the school will be coming in bought costumes like yours, with those printed-on pictures of cartoon characters. I'm going to be the only one in a costume like mine. I'm proud of it."

But when I saw what my friends were wearing, I wasn't so sure I had done the right thing by making my costume. Suzy had a dog costume that looked almost real. Darlene was wearing a ballerina costume that was absolutely gorgeous. It was all pink with a fluffy mesh skirt and rhinestones all over the top. In her hand, Darlene carried real toe shoes.

"Darlene! Your outfit. It's gorgeous!" I told her.

Darlene smiled. "Isn't it exquisite? It was my mother's favorite tutu. She was a professional dancer when she was younger, you know."

"She was? Why did she stop?" I asked.

"I was born," said Darlene. "A dancer's life

was just too difficult for a mother with a baby. Mom decided to stay home with me till I could go to nursery school. Then she got a regular job in an office so she could work normal hours. But she's gone a lot of the time this way, too."

"That's too bad," said Suzy. "My mother started working a couple of years ago, too, but only part-time. She's home by the time Barry and I get back from school."

"My mother keeps talking about getting a part-time job, now that my brothers are in first grade," I said. "But she hasn't done it yet. She's always there waiting to tell me what to do when I get home."

"Don't complain," said Darlene. "It's better to have your mother around too much than not enough, believe me."

"Oh, I believe you," I replied. "But anyhow, it was nice of your mother to let you wear her favorite ballet costume."

"Well, she didn't exactly let me," said Darlene. "I sort of took it."

"You took it?" gasped Suzy. "Without asking?"

"I had no choice," Darlene explained. "Mom was busy all weekend. Every time I brought up the subject of a costume, she started talking about something else. Then last night, when I was determined to have her listen to me, no matter what, she had this emergency business meeting. She didn't get home until after I was asleep. So what could I do? I figured I would just wear the costume to school today, then hang it back in the closet. What could happen to it in a few hours at school?"

"Nothing," Suzy and I agreed. Because at that time we had no idea.

Darlene caused quite a stir when she walked into the room. The boys whistled and howled as if they had never seen a tutu before. And some of the girls came out with really nasty remarks.

"She looks more like an overstuffed cow than a ballerina." That was from Lisa, who looked just gorgeous in a silver fairy costume with a sparkling headdress.

Darlene came right back at her. "And you're the first fairy I've seen who's built like a toothpick." It was great to see Darlene stick up for herself. She was getting some confidence.

The party moved along. We ate our candy corn and apples and drank punch. Then Mrs. Leon came up with one of her ideas to stimulate our creativity. We would each put on a little performance to act out what our costume was supposed to be.

Actually, it started out pretty well. Suzy acted like a puppy begging for a bone. I acted like a raging dragon and attacked Marvin. Harley and Ken, dressed as knights in armor, put on a fake duel. Then it was Darlene's turn. She put on her toe shoes and started dancing like a real ballerina.

She looked pretty good, too. She had this faraway look in her eyes. I had this feeling she was pretending to be her mother dancing in front of a real audience. She whirled around the room and raised her arms above her head before taking her final bow.

That's where Darlene made her mistake. No sooner had she lifted her arms than this snickering broke out in front of the room. Then Mean Marvin called out, "Look at Darlene's armpits. They need a shave!"

The whole class laughed out loud at that. Everyone saw that under Darlene's arms were sprouts of hair almost as red as the hair on her head.

I don't think any of the rest of us had hair under our arms yet. Darlene was the only one, and now the whole class knew it. How embarrassing for her. How miserable of Marvin.

Darlene dropped her arms. Her face was as red as her hair. She was embarrassed, that was for sure, but she was angry, too.

"How dare you, Marvin?" she said, her eyes flashing. She stalked over to where he was sitting, grabbed his cup of punch, and poured it over his head.

It was wonderful to see. Marvin sat there, his black cat makeup running down his face.

He deserved what he got, and he should have left it right there. But not Marvin. Not mean, miserable, monstrous Marvin. He reached out and grabbed Jeff's punch and poured it all over Darlene.

Now it was Darlene who was a mess. Punch dripped all over her face and hair. But the worst was that there was now punch all over her mother's tutu.

"Darlene! Marvin!" Mrs. Leon's voice rang out. "You two stop that right away! Marvin, that was a terrible thing you said to Darlene. Not that she should have thrown that punch on you, but you did antagonize her. I want you to apologize to each other and clean up the mess you made."

"Sorry, Darlene," Marvin mumbled. He grabbed some napkins and started dabbing away at the spilled punch. He even offered some napkins to Darlene.

But Darlene didn't respond. She stood where she was, as if frozen in place. She had this awful look of horror on her face.

Finally, her eyes focused on the napkins. She took them and began to dab the punch droplets from the tutu. The napkins soaked up the wetness, but they didn't take out the stain. A trail of red marked the path the punch had taken down the front of her mother's favorite ballerina costume.

"My mother's tutu . . . She'll never forgive

me." I could barely hear Darlene say the words. Her face got white. Then, as if in a trance, she went to the door, opened it, and left the room.

"Darlene! Come back!" Mrs. Leon called. It was too late; Darlene was already gone. Mrs. Leon looked at Suzy. "Suzy, you go after Darlene right now. Tell her I excuse her and walk home with her. There are only a few minutes left of school anyway. The rest of you help clean up this room before the bell rings. And, Marvin, you stay after everyone else. You and I need to have a little chat."

It was a subdued class that went to work straightening up the room. Everyone felt awful about what had happened. I felt especially bad. After all, I knew the whole story about how much the tutu meant to Mrs. Mason and how Darlene had taken it without permission.

I didn't wait to walk home with anyone after school that day. I didn't even wait to enjoy the sight of Marvin sitting there waiting to get his lecture from Mrs. Leon. As soon as the bell rang, I raced out of school and straight to Darlene's building. I found her apartment number on a mailbox, took the elevator up to the fifth floor, and rang the doorbell.

"Who is it?" I heard Darlene say through the door.

"Linda. Will you let me in?"

The door opened a crack. "Oh, Linda. Well,

I guess you may as well come in, too. Suzy's here, and as long as I'm breaking rules, I'll just break a few more." Darlene opened the door the rest of the way, and I followed her inside. I noticed she had changed out of the tutu.

Darlene led me past a large living room, a dining room, and her parents' bedroom before we got to her room. I held my breath when I saw it—it was the prettiest room I had ever been in. It was all decorated in pink and white, and everything matched. On one wall was a unit where Darlene had her own stereo system, a TV, and loads of records and tapes. What luxury!

Suzy was sitting on Darlene's bed, holding the tutu in her lap. She had a glass of water on the nightstand and kept dipping a cloth in it, then dabbing at the spots on the tutu.

"It's starting to come out a little," she said when she saw me. "But you can still see some stain."

I watched helplessly for a moment; then suddenly I had this brainstorm. "Club soda!" I said excitedly. "Do you have any club soda?"

"Probably. My mother drinks it all the time," said Darlene. "But why do you want club soda? It tastes horrendous."

"Not to drink, silly," I laughed. "It gets out stains! I remember my mother used it when my brothers spilled juice on our rug. The stain came right out.''

''It's worth a try. I'll see if I can find some.'' Darlene raced off to the kitchen. She came back with a bottle of club soda and some clean cloths.

I poured some soda on the worst stain. I let it bubble, then dabbed it off with a cloth. The stain was noticeably lighter! Encouraged, the three of us went to work on the rest of the spots. Finally, we got the tutu to where we were sure it would dry without any sign of stain.

Darlene plopped down on the bed and sighed with relief. ''Thanks, girls! You don't know how much I appreciate your endeavors. It's bad enough to have to face my mother and tell her I took her tutu without permission. At least I don't have to tell her it was ruined!''

''No, once it dries, it'll be fine,'' I said. ''Which is more than I can say for Marvin. Mrs. Leon kept him after school for a 'little talking-to.' If she gives him what he deserves, I bet he won't be teasing you like that ever again.''

Darlene grew serious. ''I don't think even Mrs. Leon can keep people like Marvin from teasing me,'' she said sadly. ''I'm just the type kids like to pick on. It's because I'm so—so big, so soon!''

I could see it was bothering Darlene to talk

about it, because tears were starting to form in her eyes. "Well, don't worry about what jerks like Marvin say, Darlene. You've got your friends who care about you. That's what really matters."

Darlene took a tissue and blew her nose. Then she looked at Suzy and me and smiled. "You know, you're right, Linda. If you've got good friends, you can get through anything."

I smiled back at her and then at Suzy. At that moment, I felt really close to them. I didn't understand it. I could hardly believe it. Darlene and Suzy were becoming as good friends to me as I had ever had.

Even though they were girls.

❧ Seven ❧

IT SEEMED THAT Halloween was scarcely behind us when Mrs. Leon announced that what we really needed to do was to start thinking about Christmas. That seemed ridiculous at first, but then she explained what she had in mind.

"Our class has been chosen to put on the school Christmas play this year," Mrs. Leon informed us. "Since we're the creative-writing class, not only are we going to perform the play, we're going to write it as well. Won't that be wonderful?" Mrs. Leon practically bubbled with enthusiasm.

"The play will take priority over your other writing assignments. After all, we are going to be performing not only for the school, but for the parents as well. They'll all be invited the last week before vacation to watch a play acted, directed, and written completely by class five-two. Won't they be proud of what you can do?"

Mrs. Leon's enthusiasm was contagious. We all murmured our approval. My mind was already racing with ideas for the play and how I was going to write myself into a starring role.

"You've got until Monday to come up with a basic outline for your plays," Mrs. Leon said. "Then I'll chose the one that's best suited for our needs. You can work by yourself or together in groups if you prefer."

As soon as she said "groups," Darlene, Suzy, and I looked at one another. We were sure the three of us together could come up with the best idea for a play.

We decided to spend the entire weekend working on our script. We would meet at Darlene's house, since she was the only one with a room of her own.

I was really curious about Darlene's parents. Who were these strange people who never seemed to be around? What did they look like to have a daughter built like Darlene?

I was surprised to find that they looked pretty much like anyone else's parents. Mrs. Mason was as short as my mother, with dark curly hair. Mr. Mason was tall and balding and had blue eyes. They both seemed very happy to have Suzy and me visiting Darlene.

"I'm so glad Darlene has found nice friends here in Washington Heights," Mrs. Mason said as she brought some popcorn and pretzels into Darlene's room for us. "I felt so bad when we had to move and take Darlene away from her friends in our old neighborhood. But you two have made it so much easier for all of us. Haven't they, Darlene?"

This conversation seemed to make Darlene feel uncomfortable. "Sure, Mom," was all she said. "Now, if you don't mind, we've got a lot of work to do."

Mrs. Mason looked hurt that Darlene obviously wanted her to leave. "Well, just call if you need anything. I'll be happy to get it for you," she said a bit sadly. I could hear her heels click on the wooden floors as she walked down the hall.

"Darlene, are you mad at your mother or something?" I asked when Mrs. Mason was gone.

"Mad? No, not really. My mother just bugs me when she puts on this big production about being so concerned and caring about my feelings. This year, since we moved and I refuse to have a baby-sitter anymore, she's worse than ever. I think it's because she feels guilty that I come home every day to an empty house."

"Oh," I said uncomfortably. For a moment I pictured what it must be like to come home to an empty house every day all by yourself. I didn't think I would like it at all. Suddenly, I felt grateful that my mother was always there for me. I even felt grateful for my pesty brothers. "Well, your mother seems okay to me," I told Darlene.

"Sometimes." She shrugged her shoulders. "At any rate, she's been trying to make it up to me by buying me things. Take a look at all my new record albums."

Darlene opened the doors of her wall unit. I was amazed to see that besides all the records out on shelves, there were more inside. I knew how long it took me to save up to buy just one album. "Wow! These must have cost a fortune!" I said.

"They did. But my mother keeps bringing me new ones. 'This is to make you feel more cheerful in your new home,' she says. But I know it's just because she feels guilty."

"Well, whatever the reason, it's great to have all those records," said Suzy. "Can we listen to them while we work?"

"Sure," said Darlene. "That's what I like to do when I work anyhow—listen to records. Especially Elvis Presley records. I find him positively inspirational!"

"Elvis Presley?" I asked. "Why him? He's absolutely ancient!"

"He's dead," added Suzy.

"Not to me," said Darlene. "There's no modern singer so feeling, so—so sensual! You just have to listen to his records a few times to know what I mean. Here, I'll play some for you."

Suzy and I looked at each other in dismay as Darlene pulled out a stack of Elvis albums. Who would listen to Elvis Presley when there were so many good groups out now? Only a weirdo like Darlene.

We were sitting on the fluffy pink rug in front of Darlene's bed. Darlene put on a record, then stretched out on the rug. She propped herself up with a pink and white throw pillow and got this dreamy look in her eyes.

"I'll tell you girls a secret if you promise not to tell," she said suddenly.

"Sure," Suzy and I answered together.

Darlene began to speak in a low, husky voice. "Listening to Elvis makes me think of Harley Silver."

"Harley Silver?" I said. "But why?"

"Because he's the most gorgeous boy in the whole class," Darlene answered. "When Elvis sings a love song, I can picture myself wrapped in Harley's arms—it's absolute ecstasy!" She sighed. "Don't you find him irresistible?"

"Well, Harley is handsome," Suzy said with a nervous giggle. "But if you ask me, Kenton Wolfson is cuter. To tell you the truth, I've pictured myself in his arms a few times. Kissing, too." As Suzy said the word "kissing," she got this lovestruck look on her face and giggled again.

I sat there looking from Darlene to Suzy in amazement. Imagining themselves in Harley's and Ken's arms. Yuck! I couldn't believe it! I mean, Harley and Ken were cute, all right. But the thought of being wrapped in their arms made me shudder. Kissing was even worse. Yuck, yuck, *yuck!*

I guess my face expressed my feelings, because Darlene and Suzy looked at me and laughed. "What's the matter, Linda?" asked Darlene. "Don't you like boys?"

"Of course I like boys," I said indignantly. "To play ball with or fool around with. But who wants to go around hugging and kissing them?"

"You will someday," said Darlene.

"You'll see," said Suzy.

"Not me," I insisted. "I won't get mushy over boys—ever!"

They giggled together and began discussing all the things they found "simply adorable" about Harley and Ken. It was disgusting.

I lay back, my head propped up on a pillow. I was a little angry about the teasing I had taken. But more than that, I felt very uncomfortable about not being able to share these feelings about liking boys with Darlene and Suzy. Was something wrong with them because they went all mushy over boys? Or was there something wrong with me because I didn't?

Elvis was singing a slow song now, something about going on loving you but not to ask him why. It was a romantic song.

I closed my eyes for a moment and imagined that song being sung to me. Not by Elvis, but by some boy my age. He was handsome, smart, funny, and good at sports. But more than that, this boy was interested in me not as someone he could play ball with but as a girlfriend. That's why he was singing this love song to me.

This strange feeling came over me. At that moment, I actually wished I had a boyfriend to go mushy over and to have him go mushy over me. I couldn't believe it!

I opened my eyes and sat up fast. "Enough of this yucky talk. We're here to get our play written, and we're never going to do it unless we get to work!"

Darlene and Suzy knew I was right. They dropped the subject of boys, and we got started on the play. I put those strange feelings right out of my mind.

Once we got into the actual writing of our play, we came up with something great. Our play was about a strike at Santa's workshop. All the little elves who helped at the workshop were very unhappy because they didn't think anyone appreciated the work they did. There were songs and toys about Santa, Rudolph, and Frosty, but there was no recognition of the elves at all.

They decided to go on strike. They stopped working. Orders kept piling up, but there was no one to make the toys. Christmas was growing closer, and Santa began to panic. How was he going to get his toys ready in time?

What he did was to enlist all the Christmas characters to help him. Mrs. Claus, Frosty, Rudolph, and all the reindeer worked day and night. Still they were far behind.

Then Mrs. Claus had an idea. All the elves really wanted was a little recognition. They would show the elves how much they were needed by making a little elf doll for every boy and girl. On the doll would be a tag saying, "This Christmas was made possible by the hard work of Santa's elves."

When the elves saw this, they were so happy they came right back to work. With the help of Frosty, Rudolph, and the reindeer, and Mr. and Mrs. Claus, everything was ready in time for Christmas.

It took us all weekend to write our play. We argued over all sorts of little changes before we could agree on the final version. But when we finished, we had something we all were happy with.

Now what we needed was for Mrs. Leon to like it, too!

❧ Eight ☙

It CAME DOWN to a close contest between our play, "The Strike at Santa's Workshop," and Steven Warshinsky's play, "The Computerization of Christmas."

Mrs. Leon loved Steven's play because it was so "technologically informative." But Steven's play had only two characters—Santa and the computer. That didn't give enough kids a chance to take part. So Mrs. Leon wound up passing by her little pet, Steven, and choosing our play.

Darlene, Suzy, and I were overjoyed. Of course, we had written our play with ourselves in mind for some of the best parts. Motherly Darlene would make a perfect Mrs. Santa, roly-poly Suzy a great Frosty, and I was primed for Rudolph. We wrote our suggestions at the end of the play.

Mrs. Leon didn't take our suggestions. She decided it would be fairer to give all the kids a chance to try out for whatever role they wanted. She scheduled tryouts for the very next day.

That night I spent hours practicing to be Rudolph. I locked myself in the bathroom so I could have privacy. I practiced making reindeer faces and reindeer noises.

I thought I did a great job trying out for Rudolph. Apparently, it wasn't good enough for Mrs. Leon. She gave the role of Rudolph to Jeff Davidson. Not only that, she gave Frosty to Steven instead of to Suzy. Darlene was the only one of us who got the role she wanted. As the biggest girl in the class, she was the obvious choice for Mrs. Santa.

Suzy and I were given roles as lowly elves. That wouldn't have been so bad, except that the role of elf leader was given to Marvin. There was no way I could tolerate being led by him, even in a play!

"That's not fair," I began to protest. But Mrs. Leon's warning glance and Suzy's cautioning hand on my arm quieted me down fast.

"If you don't shut up you'll wind up without a part at all," Suzy whispered.

I knew she was right. Mrs. Leon didn't yell and scream, but she could be very tough in order to get her point across. She was definitely capable of taking the part away from me.

Nope, if I wanted to be Rudolph, I would have to go about it some other way.

My first plan of action was to make Mrs. Leon feel I was really making an effort with this play. That way, if anything came up, she would be much more likely to give me a better part.

I began by volunteering to help with anything that needed to be done for the play. I helped develop the dialogue, typed up corrections, and ran the copy machine until my eyes were blurry from the flashing lights. When it came time to make scenery, I not only came up with the artistic ideas, but I volunteered to head the scenery committee.

This was a big job, but a lot of benefits came with being on that committee. For one thing, I liked anything to do with art, so drawing and painting were actually fun for me. Also, the committee members were excused from regular afternoon classwork so we could work on the scenery.

The scenery had to be made in two separate sections. One section showed the inside of Santa's workshop, and all inside action would take place on that part of the stage. The other section showed a snowy countryside, where all outside action would take place. This way we got to show things like the elves picketing outside while Santa worked inside.

We had managed to sketch everything out on large sheets of paper while working in the classroom. When it came time for painting, however, the classroom was too crowded.

"We'll have to go down to the auditorium so you can spread out and paint," Mrs. Leon told the scenery committee. "I'll give the rest of the class an assignment, and we'll work in the back of the auditorium. You committee people can work on the stage up front. That way one group won't disturb the other, and we can all get something done."

I had been hoping Mrs. Leon would send us committee members to the auditorium by ourselves, but of course there was no way she would allow us to go unsupervised. The arrangement she had come up with was the next best thing, however. The auditorium was big enough so that if she were busy in the back, we would be pretty much on our own up on the stage.

I was right. As long as we kept our voices down, we could fool around and have a great time while painting.

Darlene, Lisa, and Rena were working on the workshop part of the stage, along with Harley. It was funny to watch all three girls try to maneuver to work next to Harley at the same time and still not get covered with paint.

I was working on the snow scene with Jeff, Marvin, and Suzy. Jeff, who had known Suzy since she was a little girl, was joking about the way Suzy used to look.

"Do you remember the time our mothers took us to the beach together a couple of years ago, Suzy?" he asked.

"Uh-huh." She nodded unsuspectingly.

"It was a great day—except for the problem with the beach ball."

"Beach ball? I don't remember a problem with the beach ball."

"Oh, but there was. Barry and I wanted to play catch, but when I went to pick up the ball, you were there in your striped bathing suit. You were so round and roly-poly that I got confused and threw you by mistake!"

Suzy's face turned all red. "Jeff! You—you—you creep, you!" She raised her paintbrush as if she was going to throw it at him. Then she laughed good-naturedly and put it down again.

The rest of us howled with laughter. It wasn't so hard to imagine chubby Suzy being mistaken for a beach ball.

That's when Miserable Marvin decided to get into the act. "You think that's anything? You should have known Linda a couple of years ago. She cut her hair real short and wore boys' clothes so that everyone would think she was a boy. She looked like a boy all right, but there was one way we could tell she was still Linda."

"What was that?" Jeff asked.

"Her smell!" Marvin held his nose. "There was nothing she could do about smelling like Linda! Phew!" Marvin screwed up his ugly face.

I guess everyone found this very amusing, because they all laughed. I didn't find it amusing, however, not one bit. Maybe I'm not as good-natured as Suzy, or maybe it's because Marvin is much more miserable than Jeff. Whatever the reason, I was angry enough to follow through where Suzy had only made a threat.

"There's only one person who smells around here and that's you, Marvin," I announced. Then I picked up my paintbrush and threw it at his hateful, grimacing face.

My aim was excellent. The paintbrush, white from painting snow, hit Marvin in the forehead, leaving a big white streak that was beautiful to behold. Unfortunately, when the brush bounced off Marvin it landed on the scenery.

"Oooh! Look what Linda did to our work! It's positively ruined!" Lisa shrieked.

I looked and felt awful. There was now a big streak of white all over the Christmas tree and pile of presents that had just been painted. I had done the damage, but it was all Marvin's fault. If he hadn't opened his mean, fresh mouth, none of this would have happened.

"Children! What's going on up there?" I

heard Mrs. Leon call from the back of the auditorium. I turned around and saw her marching down the aisle toward the stage.

Now I was in for trouble. Once Mrs. Leon found out what had happened, she was bound to remove me from the scenery committee. I would be relegated to the back of the auditorium while my friends went on painting. I could forget about ever getting a better part in the play.

These thoughts made me even angrier at Marvin. I had blown everything now, so I might as well blow it good. I bent down to reach for the can of white paint. I had every intention of dumping the whole thing over Marvin's head.

A strong hand grasped my wrist and stopped me. "Cool it, Linda," Jeff's voice whispered. "If you do what I think you're planning on doing, we're all in for trouble."

"Okay, okay. I won't do anything," I whispered back as I shook myself loose from him. We all turned to face Mrs. Leon as she came up to the stage.

"What's going on here?" she repeated.

Everyone's eyes focused everywhere but on Mrs. Leon. No one wanted to say anything.

Finally, Jeff spoke up. "It was an accident, Mrs. Leon. Linda's paintbrush slipped and landed on the scenery. It looks kind of messy, but it's nothing that can't be fixed."

"I can see that." Mrs. Leon shook her head as she surveyed the damage. Then she looked over at Marvin. "And I know that accidents like that do happen. But will someone please tell me how Linda's paintbrush slipped and wound up painting Marvin's forehead?"

Of course nobody would. Fortunately, Mrs. Leon decided not to make an issue out of it. She let us go back to painting the scenery while Marvin went to wash his face.

I guess I should have been thankful to Jeff for having saved me, but that didn't change the basic problem. Jeff was still the one who had the role I wanted most in the play—the role of Rudolph. I still had every intention of finding a way to make that role mine.

By December, we had practiced the play so often that I knew all the lines by heart. Kids who forgot their parts didn't have to wait for Mrs. Leon to prompt them. I was always quick to call out the proper line.

There were two reasons I did this. One, of course, was to help out the person who forgot the line. The other was part of my second plan of action. I wanted to make sure that Mrs. Leon knew I had all the parts memorized. This way if anything happened to someone who was playing a main character like Rudolph, she would be sure to think about using me as the understudy.

70

I was still disappointed in my role as elf number one. Although I was on stage a lot, my lines were very limited in number. I got to call out, "Elves on strike; elves on strike," as I walked around with a picket sign. I got to tell Santa that I wanted to be the model for the first elf doll near the end. That was it.

I figured that anyone could take over my part as elf number one. But it wasn't just anyone who could learn the important parts like Frosty and Rudolph. I made sure that Mrs. Leon knew I knew every word.

This paid off one day when Mrs. Leon called me aside. "Linda, you know this play inside and out by now. Would you want to substitute for any of the major characters if someone should get sick on the day of the performance?"

Would I want to? I had to struggle to contain my joy. "Sure, Mrs. Leon. I'd do that if I had to."

After that, I began to fantasize myself in the role I wanted the most. I saw myself taking over for Jeff Davidson in the role that I had now convinced myself should have been mine all along—Rudolph the Red-Nosed Reindeer.

Of course, I realized that for me to get the role of Rudolph, something bad had to happen to Jeff. This made me feel a little guilty, especially after Jeff had saved me that day with the scenery, but I put those thoughts out of my

71

mind. After all, I didn't want Jeff to come down with a major catastrophe like a broken leg or the flu. Something short and sweet would do fine. Something like a twenty-four-hour stomach virus that kept him running to the bathroom or a quick bout with laryngitis that would make him lose his voice for the day.

Every night before I went to bed I concentrated on this fantasy. I saw Jeff in bed—for just one day. I saw myself performing as Rudolph up on the stage, the shining star of the whole play. Mrs. Leon would be so impressed that I would replace Steven as her favorite for the rest of the year.

Despite all my fantasies, when Jeff didn't show up for school the day before the play, I could hardly believe it was true. I kept watching the door to our room. One part of me was afraid that Jeff would show up and ruin my chances to get his part. Another part of me was afraid he wouldn't.

Finally, at eleven o'clock, Mr. Wohl came through the door. "Mrs. Davidson just called the office," he told Mrs. Leon. "Jeff is sick with a bad sore throat that has affected his voice. It doesn't look as if he'll be able to make it for the play tomorrow. She asked if there was someone you could send over to pick up his costume so you can have it for his understudy."

A soon as Mr. Wohl had left, Mrs. Leon looked straight at me. "Well, Linda, I suppose you heard what Mr. Wohl said. It's a pity Jeff's sick, but it's a good thing you're prepared to take his part. It would be nice if you had his costume to wear to dress rehearsal this afternoon. Do you think you could stop over and get it at lunchtime?"

"Sure, Mrs. Leon. I'll be happy to get Jeff's costume," I answered. I had to struggle not to show just how happy I really was!

Jeff lived on the ground floor of Suzy's building. I was surprised to see Jeff himself open the door. He was wearing these ridiculous brown-striped pajamas.

"You would show up just when my mother is out at the store," he grumbled in a very hoarse voice. "Come in while I find the darn costume—you're letting in a draft from outside.

I closed the door to the apartment behind me. I waited in the hallway by the front door. From there I could see into the living room where Jeff must have been lying on the sofa watching TV.

There was a rumpled blanket on the sofa. On the coffee table I could see a thermometer, a pitcher of juice, and a big box of tissues. All the signs of a bad cold, I noted with satisfaction.

73

Jeff returned carrying a shopping bag. "It's all in here," he announced sadly, handing the bag to me.

I looked at his red and runny eyes and felt sorry for him. It must have been horrible for him to be sick and miss the play. But then I remembered that Rudolph was the role that should have been mine all along. "Hope you feel better, Jeff," I did manage to say.

"Yeah, I bet you do. After the play is over," he croaked. "But I might show up tomorrow just to spite you. Now, get out of here!"

He opened the door and practically shoved me out into the hall. Any sympathy I might have felt for him faded fast. Jeff deserved not to be in the play!

Much to my relief, Jeff was still absent the following morning. The play was scheduled for after lunch, so we spent the morning making last-minute preparations. We laid out all the props and carefully examined the costumes. We placed the scenery at the proper angles. Then we went through our last rehearsal and were as ready as we ever would be.

I have to admit I was great as Rudolph. As soon as I put on the costume, I was instantly transformed. Linda Berman no longer existed. In her place stood a red-nosed reindeer.

I no longer walked—I pranced. I no longer talked—I made whatever it is you call reindeer sounds. I was far better than Jeff ever could have been as Rudolph.

"Rudolph the Red-Nosed Reindeer," I kept singing when I went home for lunch.

"I don't think I've ever seen you as excited as you are over this play," my mother commented as she took away my half-eaten lunch. I really was too excited to eat.

"I know," I said. "That's because I was lucky enough to get this part. It's the one I wanted all along." Then I started singing about Rudolph again. But this time my voice creaked.

"Linda, what's the matter?" my mother asked immediately. "Your voice sounds hoarse to me."

"Hoarse? Me?" I swallowed hard. My throat did feel a little sore. But just a little. "It's nothing, Ma. Probably just the strain from all that practicing we've been doing."

But even as I said this, my throat started hurting more.

"Stop that unnecessary singing. Save your voice for the play," my mother said to me before I left for school. So as I walked back, I didn't sing "Rudolph" out loud. I just repeated the words over and over in my head. But I lost all desire to sing when I entered our classroom. For there, sitting on a chair by Mrs. Leon's desk, was Jeff Davidson.

He gave me a big grin. "Hi, Linda," he said

in a voice that while still husky, could be heard across the room. "Isn't it amazing what antibiotics can do? I got better!"

I gazed from him to Mrs. Leon. "Uh—what are you going to do?" I managed to ask. But my voice now had a decided creak in it.

Mrs. Leon looked at me sadly. "Well, Linda, this is a tough situation. I know how much you wanted to play Rudolph, and you certainly were very good at it. But Jeff was very good, too, and the fact remains that you're the understudy and the role is his. Since he fortunately is feeling better and did show up, we'll have to go back to the way it was. Jeff will be Rudolph and you'll be elf number one. I hope you can accept that."

She hoped I could accept that! How could Mrs. Leon say those words so casually when she was talking about the biggest disappointment of my life? I had worked so hard on writing the play, on memorizing all the lines. My mother and brothers were coming to see me in a starring role, but I had been relegated back to a lowly elf. It wasn't fair!

But what could I do? I could see Mrs. Leon wasn't going to change her mind. "I can accept it," I forced myself to say with a voice that sounded much like a frog's.

The play went off really well, even without me in a starring role. I managed to croak out my few lines. Jeff was wonderful as Rudolph and received a big round of applause.

The play went well, but I felt lousy. Maybe I deserved what had happened because of all the evil thoughts I had sent out to Jeff. But the fact still remained that I had a sore, hoarse throat.

"Thank you for being such a wonderful audience," Mrs. Leon announced when the applause for the leading characters died down. "I just want you to be aware that besides the characters you saw on stage today, there were some very important people working behind the scenes. This entire play was written by three members of our class—Darlene Mason, Suzy Kletzel, and Linda Berman. Girls, will you come up and take a bow?"

Surprised, Darlene, Suzy, and I scrambled to the front of the stage. We had recognition! My dark mood was lifting fast.

It disappeared completely a moment later when Mrs. Leon added, "I want to give special thanks to Linda. She managed to perform her part as elf number one despite a big disappointment and a very hoarse voice."

Beaming, Mrs. Leon stretched her hand out to me. I stood there open-mouthed until Darlene gave me a poke and whispered, "Take another bow, dummy." I stepped forward and bowed, basking in that special applause just for me. It was wonderful!

When I walked back to the rest of the group,

Miserable Marvin scrunched up his face and stuck his tongue out at me. I felt too good to care.

I even felt too good to care when Jeff whispered to me, "You're going to be sick and suffering all vacation long!"

✺§ Nine §✺

JEFF WAS RIGHT. I did suffer from the throat infection he passed on to me. And the antibiotics didn't work so well with me. It took almost half my vacation to get over it.

During this time we had the first substantial snowfall of the winter season. Snow, the only thing that made winter bearable, and I was too sick to go outside!

I was miserable. As I sat by the window, watching everyone else having fun in the snow, a snowball came crashing into the window-pane. I looked down and saw Jeff grinning up at me from the street.

"To-o-o bad you're sick and can't come out, Linda," he taunted me. He ran away, laughing, before I could do a thing.

That moved Jeff right up there next to Marvin on my list of people I disliked the most. I was on the lookout for a way to get even with him.

I didn't see him again during vacation. I decided against trying anything at school. Mrs. Leon seemed to be feeling better about me after the play, and I didn't want to do anything to ruin that. So I kept waiting for the time to be right.

My opportunity to get even arrived at the beginning of February. That's when we had the next big snow.

I sensed it coming the night before. The first flurries began to fall from a sky that was heavy with snow-filled clouds. You could feel it in the air, taste it on the wind. This storm was going to be a big one.

I ran to the window as soon as I woke up in the morning. What I saw made me gasp with joy. The dull gray city had been transformed as if by magic into a sparkling white winter wonderland. The snow was deep enough so the schools would be closed for sure. I couldn't wait to get to the park with my sled!

Unfortunately, neither could my brothers. My mother insisted I take them with me. It didn't matter that I had arranged to meet Darlene and Suzy. There was only one sled in our family. If I wanted to use it, I was stuck with Ira and Joey.

We met in the back of the park at the big hill that everyone used for sledding. Darlene and

Suzy were there when I arrived. I was relieved to see Suzy's brother, Barry, there sharing her sled. At least I wasn't the only one stuck with little brothers.

Suzy had a great idea: we would let our brothers use our sleds, and we would share Darlene's so we could be left in peace.

That worked out well. Darlene, Suzy, and I piled on Darlene's sled, three at a time. The last one on got to push off, then take a running jump to land on top of the others. We would all whiz down the hill and wind up in a laughing heap at the bottom.

I was having a terrific time. I thought Darlene and Suzy would be, too. But they kept looking around impatiently as if they expected someone else to show up.

Sure enough, someone did. First we spotted Sue-Ann and Lisa, racing up to the top of the hill. After them came a cloud of flying snowballs. After the snowballs came the boys—Harley, Ken, Jeff, and Marvin.

Darlene and Suzy lit up when they saw the boys. I realized that's who they'd been waiting for all along.

"Help! Help!" Sue-Ann and Lisa yelled when they saw us.

Darlene and Suzy exchanged glances. They saw their chance to get Harley and Ken to notice them. I saw my chance to get even with Jeff and Marvin. We abandoned Darlene's sled to my brothers. Gathering up armloads of snow, we charged right into the midst of the action. Snowballs were flying everywhere.

We girls had the boys outnumbered five to four. We should have beaten them easily. But Sue-Ann and Lisa were next to useless. They were so busy ducking snowballs they couldn't seem to throw any.

The boys were killing us! We raced to the cover of some nearby bushes. There we were able to build up our supply of snowballs. The boys kept closing in on us just the same.

There was only one thing to do. "Come on, girls! Let's take the offensive!" I called. Grabbing an armful of snowballs, I ran out toward the boys. The girls hesitated, then followed my lead.

It was a mistake. At first, we managed to drive the boys back. But then their superior snowball-fighting ability won out.

Sue-Ann and Lisa were the first to give up. Shrieking and squealing, they ran off down the hill. Marvin chased after them, still throwing snowballs. That was just what Sue-Ann and Lisa deserved.

Darlene and Suzy stood their ground a bit longer. But they, too, were soon overcome by the attacking boys.

Before I realized what was happening, Harley had grabbed Darlene from behind, and Ken had grabbed Suzy. As the boys held Darlene and Suzy back, Jeff began pummeling them with snow.

"Stop! Help! Stop it!" Darlene and Suzy protested this attack. But at the same time, Darlene leaned back into Harley's arms as if she couldn't get enough of them. Suzy giggled and squirmed delightedly against Ken.

It took me a minute to realize what was happening. Despite their protests, Darlene and Suzy were enjoying every minute of being defeated by the boys!

Defeat was something I wanted no part of. While Jeff was busy with Darlene and Suzy, I took a pile of snow and dumped it over his head.

It was a beautiful sight to see. Snow sticking to Jeff's hair, his eyes, and his lashes. Snow dripping from his nose and chin. Snow stuffing his big mouth. He let out a muffled scream and began stomping around, trying to shake off the snow. He looked like a big hippopotamus coming out of white mud. I cracked up at the sight of him.

"That's what you deserve for getting me sick over Christmas vacation, Jeff," I laughed. "Now we're even!"

But Jeff didn't seem to agree. As soon as he had brushed the snow from his face, he started after me.

I could see he was angry, so I took off running through the snow. I would have gotten away from him, too, if I hadn't slipped on an icy spot and fallen to my knees.

That was the chance Jeff needed. He took a flying leap and landed on top of me. It was a very awkward position to be in.

Unfortunately, it was at that moment my brothers decided to investigate what I was doing. When they saw me lying under Jeff, they found it very entertaining. They immediately started making stupid remarks.

"Oo-ooh! Look at Linda and Jeff! They must be kissing! Linda and Jeff, k-i-s-s-i-n-g! Linda's got a boyfriend!"

"I have not!" I managed to pick up my head and say. "I'm a tomboy! I do not have a boyfriend. I will not ever have a boyfriend. And even if I did, the last person on earth I would choose is fat, disgusting Jeff Dav—oof!"

The "oof" was because Jeff had just used his fat, disgusting hand to push my face down into the snow. My first reaction was anger. This soon changed to fear when I realized I couldn't breathe like that!

I tried to tell him, but all that came out was a muffled "wwhmph!" I began gasping and choking, but he still pushed down on my head!

Panic overtook me. With it came a strength I didn't know I had. With a sudden burst of energy, I squirmed from Jeff's grasp and rolled over on my back. I brought up my knee, which connected with Jeff's stomach.

That got him off me fast. "Ow-ooh!" he bellowed, grabbing himself where it hurt. He made so much fuss that Harley and Ken let go of Darlene and Suzy and ran to Jeff's assistance.

"Run, girls, run!" I yelled, taking advantage of this opportunity. We took off as fast as we could over the field of snow.

I looked back and saw Jeff had recovered enough so the boys were coming after us again. They looked really angry now. We had a head start, but they were bound to catch up to us. What were we going to do?

Suddenly, I saw the answer. "Run to the ladies' room! They can't follow us in there!"

The ladies' room was in a small building about a hundred feet away. We raced for the building and made it there before the boys could get us. We ran inside and slammed the door.

A quick glance around the bathroom assured us it was empty. We locked the latch and leaned against the door, gasping for air.

When our breath had returned, we all looked at one another and cracked up. What a mess we were, soaking wet and dripping snow! We pulled off our wet hats and gloves and put them on the radiator to dry.

"Wasn't that the most delectable experience?" Darlene gushed as she warmed her hands over the hissing steam.

"What do you mean, delectable?" I demanded. "Neither one of you would have escaped from Harley and Ken if they hadn't had to come to Jeff's rescue."

"So, who wanted to?" said Suzy. "I could have remained in Ken's arms forever!"

"Being enveloped by Harley was pure ecstasy!" added Darlene.

"Ecstasy?" I repeated disgustedly. "You two missed the point completely. We met the boys head on in a test of strength and skill, and we emerged victorious. That's what's important!"

"Victorious? How do you figure that?" asked Darlene.

"Because the boys are out there in the cold while we're safe and warm right here," I stated proudly.

But even as I said that, we heard this horrible banging on the bathroom window. The glass was frosted so you couldn't see through, but you could hear through it fine.

"We heard what you said about emerging victorious." It was Jeff's voice we heard first. "You might be safe and warm right now, but you've got to come out of there sooner or later!"

"And we'll be right here waiting for you when you do!" Ken's voice added.

"So you might as well come out now," said Harley.

"Come out, come out, wherever you are!" That was Marvin's voice. So he was waiting for us now, too.

More banging on the window. Then I heard my pesty brothers' voices. "Linda! Come out of there! Linda, we're cold. We've had enough sledding. We want to go back home!"

As if that wasn't enough, someone began banging on the door. "Hey, who locked the door to the ladies' room? Open up! We have to go in!"

"What are we going to do now, Linda?" Darlene and Suzy were looking at me as if this whole mess was my fault.

I was struggling to come up with an answer, when suddenly all banging and shouting ceased. A key turned the latch from outside, and the door swung open. There in the doorway stood Mr. Mancuso, the park attendant, his face flushed with anger.

His eyes scanned the bathroom—the hats and gloves draped over the radiator, the piles of melting snow that had dropped from our jackets, the mud-streaked footprints all over the bathroom floor. Then his eyes focused on me.

"You again!" he roared. "How come whenever I see you, you're causing trouble?"

"B-but I didn't do anything!" I protested. "All I wanted was a nice day of sledding. Then the boys came along and chased us in here, and they want to kill us! That's why we had to lock the door."

"Who-oa! You're telling that story way too fast for me to follow," said Mr. Mancuso. "But whatever happened, you can't keep people from using the rest room." He stepped aside to let in the girls who had been banging on the door.

"I'll tell you what. I'll send those boys home and make sure they don't bother you again. But first"—he produced a mop and stuffed it into my hands—"you clean up this mess you made on the floor!"

"Me? But I didn't—" I began. But one look at Mr. Mancuso's face told me there was no use protesting. I took the mop and cleaned up the floor while my brothers looked on gleefully from the open doorway.

I guess Mr. Mancuso scared the boys off, because we all got home safely that day. The snow melted over the weekend, and I thought the incident was over and forgotten.

But then, two weeks later on Valentine's Day, the strangest thing happened. We had a little party in school, and Mrs. Leon gave out the Valentines our class had stuffed into this box decorated with big hearts. She handed me a very weird Valentine.

Instead of being red and heart-shaped, it was

white and shaped like a snowball. Inside was written in big letters:

> *Snowballs are white*
> *But turn you black and blue.*
> *Did you know that tomboys*
> *Can fall in love, too?*

I was sure Darlene or Suzy had sent me the card to tease me, but there was another card from them. It was written like an addition example:

$$
\begin{array}{r}
2 \text{ Young} \\
\underline{2 \text{ Go}} \\
4 \text{ Boys}
\end{array}
$$

Inside were written the names of the boys—Harley, Ken, Jeff, and Marvin, and hearts were drawn all over. Typical of Darlene and Suzy's sense of humor.

They both swore to me that this was the only Valentine they had sent me. So the other one had to be from one of the boys who were in the park the day of the snowball fight.

But which one? And why? I didn't understand it at all.

❧ Ten ❧

VALENTINE'S DAY WAS about the only break we had between Christmas vacation and Easter. Mrs. Leon kept us busy with one assignment after another. It was social studies reports, science experiments, math, spelling, and English, day after day.

Mrs. Leon claimed she was really doing us a favor with all this work. It would prepare us for sixth grade, which was going to be really tough to prepare us for junior high. And, of course, junior high would be even harder to prepare us for high school, which was going to prepare us for college.

Looking at it that way, it seemed as if we were going to be in school forever. The thought was overwhelming. I decided the best thing was to just get through one day at a time. But each day brought work, work, and more work!

About the only thing we had to look forward to was Friday afternoons. That's when we put the rest of our work aside to develop our storytelling project. We had spent the first part of the school year writing our stories. Now we had to illustrate them and get them ready to present to the first and second grades.

I figured that the storytelling project would be a perfect way to finally get Mrs. Leon to appreciate me. Since writing and drawing were two of my strong points, I had a great story all ready for the first week of story hour.

I could picture myself making such an impression on the first- and second-grade teachers that they would come and tell Mrs. Leon what a great job I had done. Finally, Mrs. Leon would realize my worth. Finally, I would become her favorite instead of Lisa and Steven Warshinsky.

"Steven Warshinsky—Linda Berman!"

I emerged from my daydream hearing my name paired with his. It took me a moment to realize what was happening. Mrs. Leon was reading off her list of kids she had placed together to present their stories. She had paired a boy with a girl whenever possible. I noticed Darlene had wound up with Harley and Sue-Ann with Jeff, on whom she had developed this mad crush. But it was just my luck to wind up with Steven Warshinsky, the little creep!

I was about to protest, then thought better of it. This might be the very opportunity I needed. Seeing us working together might be just the thing to make Mrs. Leon realize that, when it came to writing at least, I was way ahead of Steven.

Mrs. Leon told us each pair of students could decide for themselves whose story would be presented on this first Friday. After that, we would keep alternating stories.

As far as I was concerned, my story *had* to be first. I was afraid that after the little kids saw how boring Steven's stories could be they would ask their teacher not to let us read to them again. Then I would never get to do my story and impress Mrs. Leon.

I told this to Steven, but I guess that wasn't the best approach to take. It only made him more determined to do his story first.

"Everyone knows my stories are superior to yours, Linda," he argued. "After all, my brain is superior."

"Maybe—when it comes to adding numbers in your head. But when it comes to things human beings are interested in, you've got about as much feeling as any other machine— none at all!"

"My story about the computer who took over the world has lots of feeling! The kids are bound to like it better than your story about a kitten who ran away.''

''Only if they have a bunch of screws and microchips for a heart the way you do!''

We could have gone on like that indefinitely if Mrs. Leon hadn't asked us which story we had decided on. She shook her head when he told her we still hadn't made up our minds.

''In that case, I'll have to decide for you,'' she said. ''Steven, you do your story this week. Linda, you go next.''

I was furious! This was a perfect example of why I had to replace Steven as Mrs. Leon's favorite. She always picked him first for everything.

To make things worse, Mrs. Leon assigned us to Mrs. Flynn's first grade. That was my brother's class, and that meant everyone would know who I was. I would never be able to live down being associated with Steven's dumb story.

I came up with a solution to the problem. I told Steven if we were going to put over his story we should jazz it up a little by acting it out. He would play the role of the boy genius who figured out how to operate a computer by cracking its code. I would play the role of Compto the computer who started out doing what the boy wanted and wound up having a mind of its own.

93

I figured that I could make a computer mask to put over my head. I could disguise my voice to make computer sounds. Then no one would know who I was.

Much to my surprise, Steven agreed to my plan. I guess maybe he didn't want anyone to know who I was, either. After all, he liked his own story and wanted all the glory for it. Well, as far as I was concerned, he was welcome to that kind of glory!

I made my mask late at night so my brothers wouldn't see me working on it. I found a carton that just fit over my head. I pasted on gray construction paper and buttons and bottle caps for knobs. I cut out holes for the eyes and mouth.

"Now, remember," I told Steven before we walked into Mrs. Flynn's room. "Just refer to me as your assistant, not by name."

"Suit yourself," he said with a shrug. "I know the kids are going to love this story."

"I'll bet," I said sarcastically. I slipped on my mask. It was a tight fit. I should have cut out a section for my nose which was squashed against the box. But at least my eyes could see and my mouth could talk. And no one would be able to recognize me.

I couldn't believe it, but it turned out that Steven was right. There was something about the computer story that appealed to the first-grade mentality. Probably my portrayal of the computer had a lot to do with it. Whatever the reason, the kids kept laughing all through the story. At the end they gave us a big round of applause.

"Wonderful job, Steven—and assistant." Mrs. Flynn beamed at us. Then she stared at my computer head. "Well, Compto, aren't you going to show us who you really are?"

I was going to refuse. Then I figured, what did I have to lose? The story was a big success. Mrs. Flynn was bound to tell Mrs. Leon what a great job Steven did. I might as well get some credit for it, too. I put my hands up to my mask to pull it off. I pulled and pulled, but the mask wouldn't budge.

"What's the matter, dear? Are you having a problem?" Mrs. Flynn asked worriedly.

"Oh, no. It's just that the mask is a little tight," I answered. "It came off when I tried it on at home. Maybe if Steven helps me pull. How about it, Steven?"

"I don't know, Compto," wise guy Steven answered. "You seemed to be pretty independent when you tried to take over the world. How come you need me now?"

Steven sounded very pleased with his own wittiness. The first graders laughed. Inside my mask, I was fuming.

"Come on, Steven. Enough joking. Help me off with this thing!"

"Who's joking?" said Steven. "You're the

computer. Can't you figure out a way to help yourself?''

"Yeah, Compto! You can do it! You're smarter than he is!" The first graders shouted out encouragement.

It didn't help. Try as I might, I couldn't get that darn box off my head. The more I struggled the tighter it got. The first graders kept laughing and shouting. I got madder and madder.

I forgot about impressing Mrs. Flynn. I forgot about looking cool. "Steven!" I shouted. "Get me out of here before I wring your square little neck!"

The first graders roared with laughter, but Mrs. Flynn was not amused. "Children!" she said in a shocked voice. "This is no way to behave in front of little first graders. Mrs. Leon sent you here to be a good example, you know. Now, Compto, you come here and let me see if I can get that mask off. Or else I'll have to speak to Mrs. Leon about the advisability of the whole storytelling project."

Mrs. Flynn's threat worked. I couldn't take the chance of her talking to Mrs. Leon and ruining the storytelling project. I walked over and allowed her to attempt to remove my mask. She had to cut the back open with her scissors to get it off, but at that point I didn't care. I never wanted to see that Compto mask again!

Once I was unmasked, I stood in front of the

class feeling totally naked. And once the first graders saw who I was, the shouting started all over again.

"Look! Compto is a girl! That's just not any girl—it's Ira and Joey's big sister! It's Linda Berman!"

"Oh. Linda Berman. That explains it. I've heard about you," Mrs. Flynn said. She gave me a look that was far from approving, and I decided against asking her what she had heard.

I knew when I'd had enough. Forget about using story hour to impress Mrs. Leon. I tucked what was left of my Compto mask under my arm and headed for the door.

"So long, kids. Thanks for being such a great audience for my story," Steven said proudly.

I said nothing. I just wanted to get out of Mrs. Flynn's room before anything else could go wrong.

I had almost made it when this little girl who sat right by the door grabbed my arm. "So you're Ira and Joey's sister," she giggled. "I just think they're s-o-o-o cute!"

S-o-o-o cute? Ira and Joey? I couldn't believe it! And to think this girl was only in first grade! I could imagine what she would be like when she got to fifth grade. Probably mushier than Darlene and Suzy!

Mushiness was all around me. I couldn't escape it. What was a tomboy like me to do?

* * *

Walking home with Darlene and Suzy that afternoon made me feel even worse. That was the time they picked to tell me about the latest plans for Suzy's birthday party.

Suzy would be turning eleven in April. She, Darlene, and I had been talking about how to celebrate the occasion for some time now.

Originally, we had hoped to have a party when Darlene turned eleven in January. However, her parents had been in the middle of decorating the apartment and had taken Darlene out to a fancy restaurant instead. So now we had been talking about trying to get Suzy's parents to agree to a party for her birthday.

Obviously, Darlene and Suzy had been doing some planning behind my back. From what they told me now, it seemed to be all set. Suzy's parents had already said yes to a party. But this was not to be just any party.

"What we're going to have is an authentic coeducational party," gushed Darlene. "That means boys, music, dancing—the whole works! Not only that, but you can forget boring kid-stuff kind of games like Pin the Tail on the Donkey. We're going to get the boys to play Spin the Bottle!"

"Spin the Bottle? What's that?" I asked.

"A kissing game," giggled Suzy. "Everyone sits in a circle and you spin a bottle in the middle. Whichever boy it points to is the one you kiss."

"Kiss?" I repeated in horror. "Are you crazy? The boys will never agree to that. Dancing is bad enough, but when it comes to kissing games, the boys will feel just as I do—yuck, yuck, *yuck!*"

"Maybe they'll feel that way to start out with. But we'll soon change their thinking." Darlene got this dreamy look in her eyes.

It made me sick. Suddenly I wasn't so sure I wanted anything to do with this party. I said so.

"Oh, come on, Linda. Don't be so immature," said Darlene.

"Yeah, Linda. After all, it is my birthday," said Suzy.

"I know, I know," I grumbled irritably. Now I was really upset. This party was something I had been looking forward to, but now everything had changed. Why had Darlene and Suzy made all these plans without consulting me? Plans they knew I wouldn't be happy with at all?

✠§ Eleven §✠

As it got closer to the time of Suzy's party, I felt worse and worse. The party had become a symbol of the big difference in thinking between my friends and me. To me, a good party meant good food, good games, and good prizes. At first, I thought Suzy and Darlene agreed with me. But now it was becoming all too clear. To them, a good party meant a chance to get mushy with the boys. Yuck!

There was another thing bothering me about the party. The guest list. Of all people, Suzy had decided to invite Sue-Ann and Lisa. As for boys, Harley, Ken, and David, this other boy from our class, were fine. But because Suzy's mother was friends with Jeff's and Marvin's mothers, she insisted we invite them as well. That meant almost half the party would be kids I could very well do without.

I could have lived with all this, but then Suzy came up with the real killer. She decided she wanted her party to be formal. That meant we all had to dress up.

This was probably no problem for the other girls. But as a practicing tomboy whose basic wardrobe consisted of a meager collection of jeans and shirts, to me it was a disaster!

I went into my parents' closet, where I kept my few better clothes. There wasn't much there.

First I pulled out my one dressy dress. It had been bought for my cousin's wedding last year. The blue color was pretty and brought out the blue of my eyes, but the dress was covered with ruffles and frills. That was okay for a wedding where the only people to see me were family, but I could never wear it to a neighborhood party. It would absolutely ruin my tomboy reputation!

Next I tried on my matching pants outfit. That had always been a favorite because I could be dressed up in it and still get away with wearing pants. But now I noticed the color was beginning to fade. And I guess I had grown since I wore it last, because the pants and sleeves were both too short. I couldn't wear my pants outfit to the party, either. I had nothing to wear at all.

"Ma!" I bellowed in desperation.

"What is it, Linda?" My mother came in looking worried.

"Suzy's party is coming up, and I've outgrown my favorite outfit. I've got nothing to wear, Ma. Nothing!"

My mother looked at me, standing with my ankles and wrists hanging out of my outfit, and she laughed out loud. This made me absolutely furious!

"It's not funny, Ma!" I felt tears of frustration burn my eyes. "I can't go to the party like this. Everyone will make fun of me!"

My mother finally managed to stop laughing. "Sorry for laughing at you, Linda. You do look funny in that outgrown outfit. But what really amuses me is that you're actually taking an interest in clothes. I can't believe it!"

"I'm still not interested in clothes—not really," I protested, trying to save some face. "It's just that I have to have something to wear to the party. Can you take me shopping, Ma? This weekend? Please!"

My mother looked at me and laughed again. "Well, I never thought I'd live to see the day when Linda the tomboy would actually ask to go shopping! But since it's so important, I'll ask Daddy to watch Ira and Joey on Saturday. You and I can go over to Alexander's and see what we can find."

"Thanks, Ma!" I gave her a quick hug. I

never thought I'd actually be looking forward to going shopping!

Of course, once my mother had me in Alexander's department store, she wasn't going to let me off so easy. Before we went up to look for my outfit, she had to stop off at the first floor to buy herself some pantyhose. Then she dragged me into the shoe department where they were having a sale on boots.

"Winter's almost over, Ma. You can buy boots next year," I tried to convince her.

"Not at these prices," she insisted, picking out an armload of size-seven boots. I don't know how she managed to find so many when there were dozens of other women pulling boots off the table as if they were the last pairs on earth. Leave it to my mother; she's a born bargain hunter.

By the time she had finished trying on all those boots and standing on the long line to pay for the ones she wanted, I was exhausted. Now I remembered why I never wanted to go shopping!

"Now it's time for you," my mother announced when she finally got off the line.

"I thought that was the reason we came here in the first place," I grumbled. Right then I wasn't feeling very good about my mother.

*　　*　　*

When we got upstairs to the children's department, my mother and I had another conflict. She wanted me to buy a dress that was dressy enough for any better occasion. I wanted another pants outfit to replace the one I had outgrown. I would up trying on both.

Since you can only take three outfits into the fitting room at one time, I was at my mother's mercy. I picked out the first three outfits, but then I had to send her out to bring in other sets of three. That way I didn't have to keep getting dressed and undressed again. But I did have to stand around in my underwear, waiting for her to bring me the next batch of clothes.

It's got to be the worst feeling in the world, standing around in the dressing room waiting for your mother. At Alexander's, there are these little partitions separating one area from another, but they do nothing to give you privacy. Anyone could peek around your partition and watch you get undressed and check on your underwear.

And unfortunately, my underwear turned out to be a problem. "Linda! Didn't I tell you to put on your best underwear when you go shopping or to the doctor?" my mother exclaimed when she saw what I had on.

"Uh-huh." I nodded with embarrassment. "But I was in such a hurry to get dressed this morning that I forgot. I just put on the first thing I pulled out of the drawer."

"I can tell." My mother shook her head and left to get me some more clothes to try on.

As soon as she left, I turned around to check myself in the mirror. I could have died of shame! My underpants had a big hole in the back. Through it poked a patch of pink skin from my behind!

Quickly, I pressed my back against the mirror so no one could see. But now it looked as if I was standing like that so I could watch everyone else get undressed.

The girl behind me, who already was wearing a bra, was just taking off her blouse when she spotted me standing that way. "You looking at something?" she said in a tough voice.

Normally, I would have said something tough right back. But I felt very vulnerable standing there in my ripped underwear. "N-no," I answered, sliding my back over to the side partition so I no longer was facing her. But someone else was bound to think I was staring at them. What was taking my mother so long?

I found out a few minutes later when she returned and handed me a small Alexander's bag. "New underpants," she said with a smile. "Put them on right over your old pair."

I smiled back. Sometimes my mother could actually be understanding.

I must have tried on every outfit in my size that afternoon. But it was worth it, because we finally found something both my mother and I liked. It wasn't pants, and it wasn't a dress, either. It was a skirt with a matching blouse you could wear separately if you wanted to. It was in two different shades of blue, both great for my eyes. It was dressy, but not frilly. It was perfect.

I was so happy to have found the outfit, I didn't even complain when my mother made another stop to pick out a pocketbook to go with her boots. I had no idea then that my new outfit was going to cause so much trouble.

The day of the party finally arrived. Everything was carefully planned. We had records, games, and refreshments. We didn't think anything could go wrong. So why was I feeling so nervous?

I took a shower and went into my parents' room to get dressed. Everything was laid out on the bed. My new outfit *and* my new underwear.

I slipped out of my robe and reached for my underwear. That's when I caught sight of myself in the full-length mirror on the door.

There I was, face to face with my own body. It was so unusual for me to be looking at myself naked that I actually was embarrassed.

I soon got over that feeling and began to examine myself. I was about average height for my age and not too thin or too fat. But I could see that parts of me had more weight than I wanted.

Like my rear end. When I stood sideways I could see that it curved out and in like a ski slope. I didn't like that at all.

I turned to look at myself straight on. My arms were okay, pretty muscular for a girl's. I flexed my biceps and was pleased to see the muscles bulge. And my chest was muscular, too. In fact, I could see some muscular definition that hadn't been there before.

I looked again, and this sinking feeling came over me. It suddenly hit me that what I thought was muscular definition really might not be at all. Could it be that I, Linda Berman, was starting to develop breasts?

The thought made me sick. Breasts. What would I do with them? Could I still climb trees if I had to wear a bra? Could I still be a tomboy? What was I going to do?

What I did was to cover up my body by putting on my new outfit as quickly as I could. Once I had the blouse on, you couldn't tell whether I had breasts or not.

You also couldn't tell that I was a tomboy. This year I had been letting my light brown hair grow. It now reached almost to my shoulders, and that didn't help. Anyone looking at me now would think I was just another girl, like Sue-Ann or Lisa.

Now I was sorry I had let my mother talk me

out of buying a pants outfit. There was just no way I could be comfortable in a skirt!

But there was nothing I could do about it. I looked at my watch and saw it was already time to leave for the party. I had nothing decent to change into anyhow.

I would have to go to the party the way I was and hope that no one would pay any attention to what I was wearing.

❧ Twelve ❧

I WAS THE last to arrive at the party. Everyone stared at me as I came in. No one was used to seeing me in anything but jeans. Everyone had a comment to make.

"Could that be Linda? In a skirt? Then it's true that she's really a girl?" big-mouth Marvin started right in.

"Are those really legs sticking out of there?" asked Harley.

"They look a bit bowed, but I think they're legs just the same," answered Ken.

Everyone was laughing and joking at me. I probably could have taken it if it had ended right there. But just making remarks wasn't enough for Jeff. He decided to try some physical action.

"Let's check them out and see," he said.

Then before I realized what was happening, he grabbed the bottom of my skirt and lifted it up.

"Let go of that!" I shrieked, slapping his hand until he released my skirt. He hopped around and laughed as if the show he had just put on was the funniest thing ever.

I felt my whole body fill with rage. Then, before I knew what was happening, I hauled off and punched him right in the nose.

"My nose, my nose! She broke it!" Jeff immediately began to wail. He put his hands up to his face, and when he brought them down they were streaked with blood.

When I saw all that blood I felt awful. I hadn't meant to hurt him that badly. I was just so angry for a moment. And now he was bleeding all over!

"Ooh, blood! How disgusting!" Lisa squealed.

"Poor Jeff. Are you okay?" Sue-Ann rushed to his side.

"Ugh! He's dripping blood on the carpet," Darlene pointed out.

"Here, take some napkins." Suzy grabbed a handful off a nearby table and stuck them in Jeff's face. "I'll get some ice."

She disappeared into the kitchen while Darlene got some more napkins and dabbed at the blood on the carpet. Unfortunately, the bright red stains didn't seem to fade, no matter how much she rubbed.

"Come on, Jeff, aren't you going to get her back?" Marvin tried to stir up some more trouble.

But all Jeff could do was clutch his nose and moan, "My nose, my nose!" He sank into a chair, throwing back his head dramatically.

I stood there, not knowing what to do. Here Suzy's party had hardly gotten started, and I had already ruined it. I wished I could sink down into the floor and disappear.

Suzy came rushing back out of the kitchen, carrying a plastic bag of ice cubes. After her came her mother. She stood stock-still, this look of horror on her face as she surveyed the scene in front of her.

"Why, boys and girls, what is going on here?" she said, after what seemed like a very long time.

When Mrs. Kletzel made her appearance, everyone just froze in place—Jeff leaning back in Suzy's father's armchair, Sue-Ann hovering over him worriedly, Darlene dabbing at the rug with napkins. No one said anything. Everyone looked at Mrs. Kletzel. Then everyone looked at me.

I squirmed miserably. There didn't seem to be any way to get out of this one. It looked as if I was going to have to be tough, admit my guilt, and accept the consequences.

"It was my fault, Mrs. Kletzel," I blurted out. "Everyone was teasing me about wearing

111

a skirt, and then when Jeff pulled it up I got so angry I swung at him. But I didn't mean to ruin your carpet or break his nose—honest I didn't!"

Mrs. Kletzel looked at me. Then she looked at the bloody carpet and at Jeff. He was really hamming it up—rubbing the ice on his nose, throwing his head back, moaning and groaning.

"Ruin my carpet? Break his nose?" Mrs. Kletzel shook her head. "I hardly think so, Linda. As for the carpet, someone told me this trick about getting stains out. Will you go get some club soda, Suzy?"

Club soda! I had forgotten all about that trick. I let out a sigh of relief as I saw the stain bubble away and get dabbed up by Suzy.

"Now, as for Jeff's nose"—Mrs. Kletzel walked over to examine him critically—"I happen to know that Jeff is very prone to nose-bleeds. I bet the ice has taken care of that problem already."

Sure enough, when Jeff took the ice away and wiped off the last traces of blood, his nose looked just fine. It wasn't broken at all. But that didn't keep him from looking very angry.

Mrs. Kletzel noticed that, too. "Now, children, I don't want any more fighting here today. Before this party goes any further, let's see you two make up and be friends."

I looked at Jeff doubtfully. Our whole relationship since the play had been one conflict after another. It was hard to see us ever being friends. But I felt so bad about messing up Suzy's party that I was willing to try anything.

I stuck out my hand. "Truce," I offered.

He glared at me for a moment. I was afraid he would turn around and leave me there with my hand stuck out. But then he scrunched up his face into one of his funny looks and quickly shook my hand.

"Okay, truce," he said. He grinned, and I suddenly remembered that before the problems with the play, I had thought that Jeff was basically okay. So I smiled back.

"That's better!" Mrs. Kletzel beamed. "And now that you're friends, why don't you two get the party rolling? You can start off dancing and everyone else can follow!"

"Dancing?" I said in horror.

"That's right," Mrs. Kletzel sang out. She pushed Jeff and me close together. She started the stereo. Then she went around the room getting all the other boys and girls paired off to dance.

Personally, I thought it was pretty nervy of Mrs. Kletzel to force us to dance whether we wanted to or not. But the other girls looked absolutely thrilled. And it did take the attention off Jeff and me.

"I guess we'd better do as she says," Jeff said with a feeble smile.

"I guess." I shrugged weakly.

Before I knew what was happening, Jeff was holding me in this awkward dancing position. He began sort of pushing me across the carpet.

It felt very strange. The only people I'd ever slow-danced with were my father and my cousin, at his wedding. And they knew a lot more about what they were doing than Jeff did.

Still, once we got used to it, it wasn't so bad to dance with Jeff. For one thing, I enjoyed the dirty looks Sue-Ann was throwing me. She had gotten stuck dancing with Marvin, and I knew she would like nothing better than to change places with me. This made me laugh and relax more in Jeff's arms.

That's when I realized what song Mrs. Kletzel had put on. It was one of Darlene's Elvis records—the song about going on loving you and not asking him why. The very first Elvis song I had heard playing that day in Darlene's apartment.

Once again, like it had that first day, this mushy feeling came over me. I got very weak and my legs felt wobbly. I had to lean against Jeff for support.

Once again I began to wonder what it would be like to have a boyfriend and be in love. I looked up and saw Jeff's face so close to mine, and this little shiver went through my body. This frightened me. I pulled away from him, but he didn't notice. At that moment, the record ended, and the other couples were pulling apart, too.

That dance got everyone warmed up. We had some fast dances and a few more slow ones. I danced with all the boys except Marvin. To my surprise, it was fun. Fortunately, I had no more weird thoughts about boyfriends and love.

We played a great game of charades, and our team won. Then came the food, this fantastic pizza with everything on it.

Darlene waited until after we had eaten and the boys were all in a good mood because their stomachs were full. Then she brought up the topic I'd been hoping she'd forget.

"How about a game of Spin the Bottle?"

"Spin the Bottle? Isn't that a kissing game?" Harley asked. His face was bright red.

"Uh-huh," Suzy giggled. "You spin the bottle and you get to kiss the person of the opposite sex it points to."

The boys stood and looked at one another. You could see they didn't know whether to go along with this or not.

I guess I was feeling the same way. Part of me wanted no part of silly kissing games. But part of me liked that strange feeling when I was listening to Elvis sing. That part of me was actually anxious to find out what it was like to be kissed by a boy.

As I was thinking this, Sue-Ann went over

and grabbed Jeff's arm. "Say yes," she breathed into his face. "It'll be fun!"

Somehow, watching her do this made me angry. I guess it was because her actions were so typical of the type of girl I couldn't stand. I decided the strange mushy feelings I had experienced must have been a temporary craziness. A craziness I wanted no part of!

"Kissing games! Huh! That's just for sissies," I spoke up loudly. "I wouldn't be caught dead playing kissing games."

Once I said that, the boys came to their senses. They all refused to have anything to do with kissing games.

So the party ended without any kissing. I had won a victory. I should have been feeling great.

I wasn't. The girls all made it clear that they thought it was my fault that the boys wouldn't play kissing games.

I didn't care what Sue-Ann or Lisa thought. But I did care about Darlene and Suzy. They barely spoke to me for the rest of the party.

As I got ready to leave, Suzy came up to me and said, "You know I was counting on playing Spin the Bottle to kiss Ken, Linda. How could you have ruined everything that way?"

I tried to explain that if the boys had really wanted to play kissing games, nothing I said would have made any difference. But Suzy wouldn't listen to anything I said.

Darlene was even worse. "You're a traitor to your own sex," she said angrily. "You always think you have to win on every issue. Well, this is one time when winning turned you into a loser!"

I was speechless. I didn't even know what Darlene meant by that. But before I could say anything, Darlene left the party with Sue-Ann and Lisa. The boys went off in their own group. I was left to walk home all by myself.

By the time I got home I was really feeling awful about the way the party had turned out. I wanted to be alone to think and to be miserable. But my parents were sitting in the kitchen, waiting for me to tell them all about my first girl-boy party.

"How was the party? Did you have a good time?" My mother asked right away.

I stood there deciding between a slough-off answer like, "Sure, great," or an irritated one like, "What do you care, anyway?" Then I noticed the intentness with which my parents were looking at me. Suddenly I realized they weren't just asking questions to be nosy. It was important to them that I had a good time at the party. They really did care.

That's when all the mixed-up feelings I had kept inside me all through the party came out, and I started to cry. My parents looked astonished. I ran into the living room and flung myself down on the high riser that was my bed. I sobbed and sobbed into my pillow.

When I had gotten all my crying out of me I looked up. Mom and Dad were there, sitting on the sofa, waiting for me.

"Do you want to talk about what happened?" Mom asked softly.

Suddenly I did. I started by telling them how I had almost ruined Suzy's party by having this fight with Jeff. How Mrs. Kletzel had forced me to make up with him and dance with him. How everything seemed to be going fine after that until the other girls wanted to play kissing games, but the boys and I didn't. How I won out but now the other girls were mad at me, and I wound up feeling awful.

When I finished, my parents just looked at me. Then Mom took a deep breath. "Well, Linda, I hope you learned something from all this. To start with, it doesn't pay to fight."

"I know, Ma. But everyone was making fun of me! All the other girls were wearing dresses and skirts, and nobody said anything to them. Why was everyone picking on me?"

"Because, unfortunately, you ask for it, Linda," said Dad.

My father is basically a very quiet person and doesn't say much. But when he does, it's usually worth listening to. This time, however, I didn't understand what he meant by that remark.

"I didn't ask for anything," I protested.

"Maybe not in words, but in actions," he said.

"What do you mean, Daddy?"

"I mean there are ways of asking for things without even realizing it. For example, the way you make such a fuss about being a tomboy and acting tough all the time. As a result, the kids tease you when you act like a normal girl. You set yourself up for trouble."

I thought about that for a moment. "But I don't want trouble," I insisted.

"Then why do you keep looking for opportunities to prove you can outdo everyone else?" my father asked. "Why do you feel you have to win every argument, to always be tops in everything?"

"Because—because tomboys are the greatest, and I want everyone to know it! Besides, don't you want me to be better than everyone else?"

"Not at all," my mother was the one to answer. "Beating someone else doesn't make you any better as a person. What you need to do is to be the best you can possibly be without worrying about how the other guy is doing. Or about labels like 'tomboy' or 'sissy.' You just have to be yourself and be happy. You can't do that if you're always angry and fighting."

"You just wind up fighting yourself," Dad added.

"Fighting myself?" I asked, puzzled.

"Think about it," said Mom.

"Okay," I nodded. I took some tissues from the box Mom offered me and blew my nose.

I wasn't sure I understood everything Mom and Dad were trying to tell me. But I knew one thing for sure. I didn't want to continue having fights and getting people I liked mad at me.

Darlene was right when she said that sometimes winning made me a loser. Darlene and Suzy had come to mean a lot to me, even though they were girls.

I wasn't ready to lose my friends.

❧ Thirteen ❧

I GUESS IT was because I was feeling so down about everything, but I really thought a lot about what Mom and Dad had said to me.

I knew there was truth to what they said. Because I was a tomboy, I was always trying to prove I was best one way or another. This led to nothing but trouble for me. And when you thought about it, my mother was right. It really didn't matter who was best.

If I scored 90 on a test, it was worth 90 whether Steven scored higher or lower. I didn't have to compete with him for grades if I didn't want to.

If I made a great catch playing baseball, it was still a great catch, even if Harley made a better one. I didn't have to feel like I was in a contest with him or anyone else if I didn't want to.

I didn't have to be *the* best all the time. I didn't have to climb the highest tree. I didn't have to get the lead in the play. I didn't have to write the best story or throw the hardest snowball, or show everyone that I was the world's greatest, toughest tomboy.

I didn't have to prove anything to anybody. I just had to do *my* best—whatever it took to make me feel good about myself.

It did me no good to win on an issue if I wound up getting people I cared about mad at me. Having my friends was more important than being right or being best.

Once I understood this, I made up my mind to make some changes in myself. I determined to set things right with Darlene and Suzy first thing Monday morning.

But as I walked to our usual meeting place on Darlene's corner, I felt very nervous. Apologizing was not something I was used to doing. And I didn't know just how mad at me Darlene and Suzy might be.

It was one of those bright spring mornings when everything was coming up green and the air smelled sweet and clean. No one could stay mad at anyone long on a day like this, I tried telling myself as I spotted them standing together.

But I could see right away they were still angry. I took a deep breath and got straight to the point. "I guess you're mad because I ruined the kissing games at the party."

"Correct," Darlene said icily. Suzy just nodded her agreement.

This was not going to be easy for me to do. I took another deep breath. "Well, I—uh, just wanted to—uh, apologize for that. You see, I—uh, was having these weird feelings I wasn't able to deal with at the party."

"Weird feelings? Like what?" asked Suzy.

I could feel the color rising to my face. I didn't want to say more, but I knew I had to. "Well, I was actually thinking that I might want to see what it was like to kiss a boy, after all," I admitted. "I guess I didn't know how to deal with that. So I took the easy way out by saying that kissing games were for sissies. I figured that would blow the whole thing."

"It sure did," Darlene said bitterly.

"Well, I know now that wasn't fair to the rest of you," I told them. "Especially when I knew how much you were looking forward to playing Spin the Bottle. I was wrong so I . . . well, I just want to say I'm sorry."

Darlene and Suzy stared at me as if they didn't quite recognize me. Then Suzy began to giggle, and Darlene began to smile.

"What do you know?" Darlene said. "There is a human being inside that tough-guy exterior, after all."

"There may even be a girl," giggled Suzy.

"Hey, let's not get carried away here," I protested, but mildly. "Just because I admitted to being curious about kissing doesn't mean I've turned into a sissy."

"I have a suggestion, Linda," Darlene said. "Why don't you just eliminate the word 'sissy' from your vocabulary? We'd all be better off."

"Yeah. And next time we might even get to find out what it's like to kiss a boy," said Suzy.

"Okay, it's a deal," I promised, filled with relief. I was forgiven!

As we walked to school together, I knew for sure it was true. Having friends was better than being right, being tough, or being best—any day.

I changed my attitude in school, too. I started by trying to accept the fact that I wasn't going to beat Steven for top student in our class, no matter how hard I tried. I was good in school, but Steven was one of those freaky geniuses who was always going to be better.

All Steven had in his life was schoolwork and computers. He didn't play sports or have a group of friends like I did. When you thought about it that way, I had much more than he did. I didn't have to compete with him in the one area he did best. Instead, I would try to be nice to him.

This wasn't easy for me. When we went back to Mrs. Flynn's class to do one of my stories,

Steven began by making an announcement to the class.

"Don't expect a story as great as the Compto story this time, kids. I didn't write this one, Linda did."

I didn't think Steven's remark was called for at all. Automatically, I found myself reacting to it. I had this urge to stick out my foot and trip Steven to embarrass him in front of the entire class.

Then I realized what I was doing—getting angry, trying to get even and to prove I was the best. The same kind of things that always got me into trouble.

I took a deep breath and tried to look at this differently. I told myself that Steven didn't say that remark to attack me. He said it because he thought it would make him look good. Being best in school was the only thing Steven had going for him.

When I looked at the situation that way, a strange thing happened. My anger went away. I was able to smile and go on with the story as if Steven's remark hadn't bothered me at all. I didn't make a scene, and I didn't get into trouble the way I would have if I had done something to get back at Steven.

This made me feel so good I kept on with my experiment. Whenever anyone said or did something I didn't like and I found myself getting angry, I would tell myself to stop and see if I could look at the situation differently. Most of the time I found I could.

This even worked with girls like Lisa, Sue-Ann, and Rena. I decided that if they wanted to act all mushy and silly, I didn't have to let it bother me.

If all this sounds like I was becoming perfect, I wasn't. I still had plenty of slips back to my old behavior. Usually these involved Marvin Haven. He still made me so angry that, try as I did, I found it almost impossible to see anything from his point of view. Especially when he kept pulling dirty tricks, like ramming into me on roller skates or throwing my loose-leaf into a puddle.

I had to get back at Marvin, I just had to. The next time I saw him skating, I waited until his back was turned and then shoved him to the floor. I got hold of one of his homework papers and crumpled it into a little ball.

"Now we're even," I told him each time, as if that should be the end of it. It never was. As long as I kept trying to get even with Marvin, he kept thinking of more things to do to me. I didn't know if I would ever have self-control when it came to Marvin, but I really was doing better with everyone else.

Then, in June, when the school year was almost over, the strangest thing happened. At first it didn't seem related to all these changes

I was making. But when I look back on it now, I realize it had to be.

It happened during the final game of our class basketball tournament in the gym. Mrs. Leon had set up the teams so there was a mixture of boys and girls on each one.

I was lucky enough to get on the Blue team. Both Harley and Ken, two of the best basketball players in our class, were on it. We had made the finals and were playing the championship game against the Yellow team. Jeff and Sue-Ann were both on that team. It was disgusting to watch her flirt with him whenever she could.

Personally, I think that was the reason the Yellows were losing. Sue-Ann spent more time trying to get near Jeff than she did trying to get near the basketball. Anyhow, our team was winning, 12 to 8.

That's when Jeff sprang into action. He kept away from Sue-Ann and made two baskets in a row. The score was tied and the game was almost over.

Then I got the ball. I saw an opening, dribbled my way to the basket, and got ready to shoot. Suddenly Jeff was there, his big fat foot stretched out in front of him.

Somehow I tripped over his foot. The ball bounced away, and my shot was ruined. Even worse, I went sprawling on the floor in front of the whole class.

"Clumsy!" Jeff shouted.

I could have died of embarrassment. I felt that old familiar flash of anger flood my body. I forgot about my campaign not to worry about winning. I forgot my vow not to get into fights.

"You did that on purpose, Jeff Davidson!" I said, clenching my fists.

"No, I didn't," he answered. And before I could say anything more, he reached out to help me to my feet.

I was still angry, but I took his hand anyhow. Then I felt this strange tingling sensation. I looked up into his face, and I actually shivered. I saw the cute way his hair had of curling down onto his forehead. I saw him shake back his hair and grin.

For the first time I noticed how white his teeth were. And his eyes—they were so blue! I sat there in the middle of the gym with my hand in his, staring into his eyes. For a moment I felt as if I'd been transported back to Suzy's party. I was dancing in his arms again, staring into his eyes. But this time he bent down and kissed me softly on my lips. I felt my body shiver again. Then I became aware of what was going on around me in the gym.

Marvin was standing there watching us with this big smirk on his face. Sue-Ann had turned as white as a sheet. Then Harley yelled out, "That's love for you!"

Then it hit me. Love! Was that why my heart

was beating so fast? Was that why Jeff's eyes seemed to burn through mine? Was that why my hand, still holding his, was sweating so?

I couldn't believe it. Linda the tomboy had always made fun of the mushy girls who flipped over the opposite sex. Could I really have been struck by an emotion like love?

I shook my hand loose from his and rubbed my knee. Then I looked up at Jeff again. He was still grinning. I couldn't keep my eyes off him.

Who cared what the rest of the class thought? Who cared who won the basketball game? Something had happened to me that was far more important than all that.

It turned out that Jeff's team recovered the ball. At the last minute, Jeff made this long, spectacular shot, and his team won the game. This didn't bother me at all. In fact, I decided that Jeff had played so well that he deserved to win.

I went over to where Darlene and Suzy were sitting. "Did you see that shot? Wasn't he great?" I asked.

"Who?" They both looked puzzled.

"You know. Jeff. He was so—so . . . you know—fantastic."

"Fantastic?" Darlene and Suzy looked at each other. Then they looked from Jeff to me and laughed.

"Watch out, Darlene," Suzy giggled. "I

have this funny feeling that some crazy tomboy just fell in love."

"Oh, no," Darlene said in mock horror. "And I bet she's going to fall even harder than the rest of us!"

Darlene was right. All I could think of from then on was Jeff, Jeff, and more Jeff. Finding opportunities to make remarks to him during school, to bump into him on the way home, to come across him playing ball in the park or the school yard.

I could have kicked myself for having let the whole school year go by without even appreciating that I was sitting right in front of him. What Sue-Ann wouldn't have given for that opportunity!

For I had learned something else. My new philosophy about not having to be best didn't count here. When it came to love, you had to be number one!

⋇ Fourteen ⋇

IT WAS THE last day of school. Instead of feeling wonderful at the prospect of a whole summer of freedom, I was feeling awful at the thought of not seeing Jeff.

For Jeff's final composition of the year, he had written about how he was going to camp for the whole summer. Mrs. Leon had hung his paper on the bulletin board as an example of "most improved writing skills."

That composition was still hanging up. I kept going over it, rereading the words, and feeling miserable.

I was feeling particularly low as I cleaned out my desk of all the papers and junk that had accumulated there all year long. I was angry at myself because by being stuck on proving I was this tough tomboy all year, I had missed the perfect opportunity to get Jeff to like me.

This year I had sat right in front of him and had gone nowhere. Next year I might not even be in his class. And what if I wasn't and Sue-Ann was? That would be too much for me to bear!

If only I had some sort of sign that he liked me even a little. Something that would get me through the long summer until we could be together again.

As I was thinking this, I grabbed the last paper left in my desk. It was all crumpled up and stuck way back in a corner. It had probably been there for ages. I uncrumpled it and glanced down to see what it was.

I was right. The paper had been there for ages. It was that Valentine someone had sent me way back in February. On it was that silly poem about tomboys falling in love. I read it over again, thinking about how strange it was that in a way that poem had come true.

> *Snowballs are white*
> *But turn you black and blue.*
> *Did you know that tomboys*
> *Can fall in love, too?*

As I read the words, something about the way they were written seemed familiar to me. This was a handwriting I had been seeing a lot of recently.

Then it hit me. The letters were formed just

like the ones in the composition on the bulletin board. The one that Jeff had written about what he was going to do this summer. That meant Jeff had sent me the Valentine!

My eyes opened wide with amazement. I had wanted a sign, and this was it. Jeff must have liked me, at least a little, to have written those words to me.

I turned around to look at him. As his eyes met mine, he screwed up his face and stuck his tongue out at me. I laughed, and as I did so I realized something. Sometimes, when boys and girls liked each other, the only way they could show it was to act as if they didn't. So I stuck out my tongue at him and turned away.

The next thing I knew, Jeff had taken the papers he'd gathered from his desk and dumped them over my head. Everyone around us started to laugh. At one time, this would have made me angry. But now I loved it!

Still, I couldn't let him get away with that. I scooped up an armload of papers and was about to return them to him. Then I caught sight of Mrs. Leon giving me that warning look.

At this point it really didn't matter what Mrs. Leon thought of me. But I decided to play it cool anyway.

I waited until her back was turned, and then I whispered to Jeff, "I'll get even with you,

Jeff Davidson, if it takes me the whole next school year to do it."

"I can't wait until you try," he whispered back.

I turned around quickly enough to catch the twinkle in his blue eyes. And as I looked into those eyes this wonderful feeling came over me. For this kind of getting even had nothing to do with being angry.

I knew then that no matter what class I wound up in next year, sixth grade was going to be the best year ever!

---

*To find out what happens to Linda
in sixth grade, be sure to read:*
WE HATE EVERYTHING BUT BOYS